D0912502

Borrowed Time

A Village Library Mystery, Volume 3

Elizabeth Spann Craig

Published by Elizabeth Spann Craig, 2020.

This is a work of fiction. Similarities to real people, places, or events are entirely coincidental.

BORROWED TIME

First edition. June 16, 2020.

ISBN: 978-1946227645

Written by Elizabeth Spann Craig.

With thanks to Shelly and John.

Chapter One

"A party?" I asked with a sinking feeling.

"Don't look so devastated, Ann. It's meant to be *fun*," said Luna, my much-more-extraverted coworker. "It's the perfect thing to get you out and about a little more. You know, away from the hallowed grounds of the library."

I hastily interjected, "But the hostess doesn't know me. Or, at least, I don't know her. She might not want an extra guest, especially for a house party." I figured my reasoning was pretty sound. If *I* somehow lost my mind and decided to host a house party (in my tiny cottage), I certainly wouldn't want any additional guests.

Luna smiled smugly. "I thought you might say something like that. Look: here's your very own invitation." She pulled an envelope out of her denim, fringed purse.

I slowly opened it. Sure enough, there was a colorful invitation inside with my own name on it. Grace Armstrong was the hostess and she was having a house party on the lake. The leaves were almost at their peak and would certainly be this weekend, which was likely why she'd chosen this particular date.

"See?" asked Luna. "No excuses, Ann. It'll be a blast. My cousin Roz will be there, too. You know Roz."

I nodded. Roz visited the library to see Luna sometimes and was always outgoing and seemed fun to be around. I was slowly warming up to the idea, although it wasn't exactly what I'd planned for the upcoming weekend. Those plans had involved time with Fitz the library cat on my sofa at home with a good book, some red wine, and possibly a little Chinese takeout if I was feeling wild.

"So you'll go?" said Luna, grinning. "Awesome. We can go out on the boat some, do some swimming in the pool. Apparently, she even has some sort of a games room. We need to just have a good time, relax, and purge the whole work thing out of our heads for at least 24-hours. And the best thing of all is that if my mom needs anything, I'm still right here in town. So it's a getaway without really being a *getaway*."

Luna lived with her mother, Mona, who'd had knee surgery and a few health setbacks. As far as Ann could tell, she seemed healthy and vigorous, but she knew Luna felt better when she kept an eye on her.

I scowled at the invitation. "This says the party is tomorrow."

Luna grinned at me. "I just *might* have held onto the invitation for a few days so you wouldn't have as much time to come up with an excuse not to come."

"But the hostess needed to get an RSVP from me," I said, my brow wrinkling. "She has food and rooms to prepare. Heads to count."

"I already told her you could come," said Luna, completely without remorse. "I knew you would. If anybody needs a break, it's you." She glanced at her watch. "Better run! Time to get ready for storytime."

I watched as Luna hurried off, pink hair, today in pigtails, bouncing behind her. As if aware of my thoughts, Fitz the library cat jumped up on the library circulation desk in front of me, sprawling back so he could look at my face with concern. Absently, I rubbed him. "It'll be okay, Fitz. It's just a house party with a bunch of people I don't know. What could possibly go wrong?"

Fitz purred sympathetically. He understood I usually sought out more low-key entertainment . . . the aforementioned book, cat, and sofa time. But Luna was right that I needed a break from the library. And Roz *was* a nice person. The weather was great, and the leaves were at their peak of bright beauty. What's not to like?

I glanced up as someone walked through the library's automatic doors and then raised my eyebrows when I spotted Roz, a tall woman with brown hair. This had all the hallmarks of a classic Luna ambush . . . she'd called in reinforcements to convince me to go to the party in case I'd balked.

Roz smiled at me and came right on over to the circulation desk. She was a regular patron here and not just because her cousin worked here. Her eyes twinkled at me and she said, "I suddenly have the feeling you know why I'm here."

"And it's not to pick up books you have on hold," I said with a laugh.

"Luna's already spoken to you then, I guess. Don't hold it against her . . . it's really a compliment that she's so determined you come along to this party. Are you going to be able to make it?" Roz reached over and gently scratched Fitz under his chin and he purred his appreciation.

"I wouldn't dare not to. But could you tell me one thing? I didn't have much of a chance to ask Luna about the party before she had to run off and set up for storytime. She's not planning on setting me up with anybody there, is she?"

I hated being suspicious, but if there was one thing I knew, it was that everyone liked seeing people matched up in perfect pairs like animals on Noah's ark. There'd been many well-meaning patrons and friends who'd set me up on a variety of absolutely awful blind dates. They had my best interests at heart, but the dates never seemed to work out.

Roz chuckled. "You must have been burned a lot with impromptu set-ups. Nope, there is no potential love interest coming to this party. But you might make some friends—it's a great group of people. There's only one that I'm not crazy about."

Contrarily, she'd piqued my interest. "But you usually like just about everyone." It was true. She always struck up conversations with complete strangers at the library and was good to join even our most-random library events to meet different people.

Roz grinned at me. "You're right, I do. But this guy has seriously gotten on my nerves recently. He's dating my best friend, Kelly, and they make an awful match."

"Have they been dating for long?"

Roz rolled her eyes. "Far *too* long, if you ask me. It's been one of those on-again, off-again romances for ages. Scott will do or say something totally thoughtless and Kelly will be furious. She'll break up with him and I'll take us both out for ice cream to celebrate. Then he'll call, all remorseful and penitent, and the next thing I know, they're back together again. That relationship is the pits."

"Why does she put up with it, then?" I asked curiously. It was tales like this one that sometimes made me glad I was single.

Roz said, "Good question. Kelly is smart and successful and good-looking and definitely doesn't need to deal with his crazy behavior. But, much as I hate to admit it, they do seem to have a lot in common. They both enjoy reading, so you'll have seen them in here. They read *everything*—they don't seem to have a favorite genre."

"I'm sure I'll probably remember them when I see them," I said. Sometimes patrons were friendly and would interact with the library staff and sometimes they were just running in the library to pick up a book we'd placed on hold for them. Then they'd check out their book themselves and hurry out. There were plenty of regular patrons I had only fleeting impressions of.

Roz scratched Fitz under his chin and he appeared to be in heaven. She said, "Are you super-busy right now? I can fill you in on the crowd who's coming. I bet Luna didn't do that."

I said, "No, it's pretty quiet here now and I'd love to hear more about the party." I would, actually, since it would make me feel more comfortable about being there. And Luna either hadn't had much information about the guests, or didn't think to share it if she did.

Roz settled in, lounging against the circulation desk. "Good, because Luna is probably sick of hearing me go on about the Kelly and Scott situation and it's not as if I can talk about it with Kelly, you know? Anyway, they *do* have stuff in common. They like to go on walks. They like classic films. They love to read. Scott's very intellectual and went to one of the Ivy League schools and Kelly says they always have great conversations. But they also fight like cats and dogs."

I said thoughtfully, "I wonder if the hostess knows the type of relationship they have. It could make for a lot of drama for a house party, especially if they blow up at each other a lot."

Roz said, "That's what I was thinking. So, the woman hosting the party is Grace Armstrong. I've known all these folks for a while . . . we went to high school at the same time. Grace moved away for a while, married some rich guy, and then he had a sort of tragic death."

He must have been pretty young. "An accident of some kind?"

"I think so, but I really don't remember. Anyway, Grace inherited all his assets and then decided not too long ago to move back home to be near her parents, who still live here. She said she missed the mountains, too. She rented a place locally while she was having this new house built. This weekend is sort of serving as a housewarming party for her, too."

I made a mental note of this since Luna had neglected to tell me. Without knowing Grace at all, I figured the housewarming gift I brought would most likely be the usual bottle of wine. I mentally rearranged my budget and then rearranged it back. Unless Grace was a wine connoisseur, a mid-range bottle of wine should work just fine.

Roz continued, "Grace wanted the chance to reconnect with some of the folks she'd known back in the day. Since we'd all hung out together in high school, I'm thinking she just lumped us all together and made the invites. Scott and Kelly might try to behave themselves, under the circumstances."

It was starting to sound like it might not be that restful of a weekend. But it was also sounding far more interesting than it had before.

"What do Kelly and Scott do for a living?" I asked.

"Kelly does development work for a nonprofit." Roz shrugged. "And Scott has something to do with some sort of dotcom business. It's really successful, actually. Although Scott is so slick I always wondered how solid that business really was. For a while, I think he worked with Kyle on it."

"Kyle?" I asked. The rush of names was starting to confuse me.

"Sorry—Kyle Hubbard. He was also in our same class at school and was always good friends with Scott so we hung out with him some, too. Anyway, they're still good friends and Kyle is coming this weekend, too. Kyle has always had this unrequited love thing going on."

I thought wryly that it actually appeared as though Kyle and I might have something in common. I had a thing for a neighbor of mine who apparently couldn't be less-interested. I politely asked, "Unrequited love?"

"Yes. With Felicity, who is *also* coming along this weekend, according to Grace. Well, I guess it was probably our last year of high school when Kyle started his crush on Felicity—he had another girlfriend before that. Felicity is nice, sort of quiet. She's all about spreadsheets and data. She's done really well at the bank and has gone way up the ranks, apparently."

"Has she?" The Whitby Bank's tiny little local branch didn't seem like the type of place that would even *have* ranks. From what I'd seen, there was a lone teller and a single loan officer. If there was even a manager in there, I hadn't seen evidence of him or her.

Roz laughed. "She works remotely. Well, most of the time—sometimes she has to fly to New York or Atlanta or whatnot. She doesn't work for the Whitby Bank."

"No, I suppose not," I said with a chuckle. "I can't see the Whitby Bank connected to banks in New York or Atlanta whatsoever."

"Anyway, that's the whole gang. I'm really glad you're going to be able to go, Ann. Luna thinks the world of you and she wanted a friend there. She has a *cousin* there, but that's a little different." She glanced over her shoulder and saw a father with a couple of kids walking our direction with a stack of books. "I'd better run and let you work. See you tomorrow!"

The next couple of hours went by quickly as traffic in the library picked up. A group of students came in looking for reference materials for a group project, there was a woman who asked me to help with tech support with her phone, and then a man asked for help getting started with his family tree.

I slipped off to the lounge finally, since my break was long overdue. I stifled a sigh when I saw my manager, Wilson, in there. The very appearance of Wilson, always carefully attired in his spotless suit, meant work. He was very fond of thinking up ways of promoting the library. He was also very fond of assigning those projects to me, although Luna was always hoping he'd recruit her. Somehow, Wilson always seemed to think of me first.

Sure enough, as soon as he spotted me, he said, "Ann. Good to see you. I was just thinking about some ideas I had to help get circulation numbers up."

I refilled my water bottle from the filtered water pitcher in the fridge. "Were you?" I asked in a not-very-encouraging voice as I thought longingly about the Agatha Christie mystery waiting for me to pick it back up.

He nodded and stooped in front of Fitz, who was lazily regarding him from his back on the floor. I saw Wilson absently reach for Fitz's round tummy and quickly said, "Uh, I think I'd scratch him under his chin, just to be sure."

Wilson lifted his eyebrows in surprise and I held up my hands. "Hey, Fitz is a sweetheart but most cats don't really go in for tummy rubs, no matter how tempting their tummies may appear."

Wilson took my advice and gave Fitz a tickle under his chin instead, which set him to purring.

"So, the circulation. Yes, I was thinking that Fitz could have some favorite book picks we could display around the library. Maybe we could take pictures of Fitz with the books and then display the photo with the books? We could put them on top of shelves and in the stacks. Maybe a couple at the circulation desk." He frowned in thought. "We could also make a bulletin board with all the pictures in one place."

"And Fitz's favorite books would be staff picks, I'm guessing?" Fitz was a very intelligent animal, but I was fairly certain he wasn't reading on the sly.

"That's right," said Wilson. "Maybe it would be even better if the books weren't recent releases and weren't as much in demand. Perhaps some tried and true older books."

I said, "Fitz could also have some ideas for favorite new releases, too. Maybe in a separate section."

Fitz smiled up at me as if he had some ideas.

Wilson nodded. "Exactly."

I started warming to the subject, despite myself. "And then maybe we could share Fitz's favorites on social media. Once a week, to draw it out?"

"Excellent!" said Wilson, beaming at me. "That should certainly boost our circulation numbers. Could you could get working on it tomorrow?"

I blinked at him. "I'm not working tomorrow, remember? I'm not on the schedule."

"Oh, right, right. The schedule. I suppose Luna could do it." Wilson mentioned Luna rather grudgingly. He was finally starting to warm to Luna's unique approach to the library . . . and, really, Luna's unique approach to life. He hadn't been very sure at first, but Luna had been nothing if not passionate about the children and teens' sections. And he'd seen that she'd been able to bring more young people into the library for programs and for other services.

"Except that Luna is *also* off tomorrow," I pointed out. "And both of us will be out Saturday, too."

Wilson's face was horrified. "Who's working?"

"There are several staff members here and loads of volunteers. The library will be in good shape." Part of me was secretly hoping Wilson would tell me that he really *couldn't* spare me and I'd have the foolproof excuse to miss this party—which I was still a little uncertain about, despite Roz's attempt to fill me in.

"Oh. Oh, well, that's all right then. We have some really excellent volunteers this time, don't we?" Wilson peered at me for corroboration.

"We do. As I was training them, I could tell they already knew a lot of the things I was showing them. They were regular patrons before they volunteered."

"That's all good, then. All right, I'll let you get back to it. But if you could take care of that Fitz's picks thing when you return to work, I'd be most appreciative." And he scurried back toward his office.

Chapter Two

The rest of the day passed quickly and I was home before I knew it. I'd taken to bringing Fitz home with me most nights from the library, mostly for my own comfort instead of Fitz's. He seemed perfectly content at the library, curled up in his fluffy cat bed, but I loved having him next to me on the sofa while I read or sleeping at the foot of my bed. Tonight, he watched me with a twinkle in his eye as I heated up leftover spaghetti for supper. He seemed to anticipate that he was going to end up with a little ground beef at some point in the process, which he did.

After I ate, I pulled out an overnight bag and looked at my closet. Nothing seemed to leap out at me as appropriate for a house party. I decided to start with the easy stuff and opened my drawers instead, pulling out pjs and underwear. Definitely a swimsuit and a towel, since we'd be on the lake. I got those out and then reluctantly looked at my closet again. There was a black dress I could wear in case it was a fancier party than I'd been led to believe. Although I couldn't really see Luna choosing to go to anything very fancy—or, if she did, she'd likely not dress like everyone else, anyway.

I pulled out a couple more things, knowing I was over-packing, but figuring it was better to have the right clothes with me. I glanced over and saw Fitz in the overnight bag, wide-eyed and peering mischievously out as if he was preparing to leap on me. I reached out my hand and he bumped his face against it and then resumed his play in the bag.

A few minutes later, I climbed into the bed and Fitz jumped in with me. I had my Agatha Christie book with me, *And Then There Were None*, which I was reading for the third or fourth time. But my mind was too busy and I couldn't seem to calm it down enough to focus on the story. I was wishing, illogically, that Grayson could have been one of the guests for the weekend. I thought again how tough it was to know exactly where he was coming from. I was either totally misreading his signals or he was totally not sending them out. I wasn't sure which was worse.

Finally, after a few minutes of hashing things out in my head, I was ready to hop back into the story. I realized, after I put the book down for the night and turned the light off, that a mystery about a house party with a murderer in attendance was possibly not the best choice under the circumstances.

The next morning, I drove Fitz back to the library and let him in the building and then hurried back home to finish getting packed. I got a text from Luna saying she'd come pick me up—quite possibly to ensure I showed up at all.

I gobbled down a quick breakfast, packed my toiletries up, and then heard a cheerful toot of a horn and locked up the house to join Luna.

She beamed at me and I saw that her hair was a different color than it had been the day before. She put a hand up to it. "Like it?" she asked.

The purple and green stripes wouldn't have suited everyone, but strangely, they looked really good on Luna. Or at least, they looked *right* on her. "You look amazing," I said, completely genuinely.

"Thanks. You do, too." She gave me a critical once-over before giving me a thumbs-up. "You always look beautiful, you know, but at the library you're pretty buttoned-up looking. I'm glad you're wearing something more casual."

I'd spent a lot of time figuring out what to wear, so I appreciated Luna's feedback. I ended up with a brown knit dress.

I'd never ridden with Luna before and winced as she took off at a fast clip. "Don't worry," she said in a cheery voice as I clutched at the door, "I'm a great driver."

I wasn't sure about *great*, but she was definitely a speedy driver and minutes later we were pulling into the driveway of a massive house on the lake. Luna finally came to a complete stop. "Just look at that view," she breathed.

It was pretty spectacular. The leaves were changing and creating a red and orange backdrop to the serene quiet of the lake. The house was tremendous, but somehow managed to pull off not being ostentatious. It had a nice, cabin-y feel to it, even though it was more of a mansion than a cabin. Somehow, I hadn't expected something this huge. The house was made of a dark wood with floor to ceiling windows to take in the view. The yard was scattered with hammocks and wooden benches and small flower beds to invite guests to have quiet moments outside. The mountains were right past the trees bordering the lake and looked so close that it almost looked as though you could touch them.

Luna grinned at me. "This is gonna be fun. Thanks for coming with me."

She drove to the bottom of the long driveway. Although we were right on time, it looked from the number of cars there as if everyone else had already arrived. There was lots of room to park, though, without blocking anyone.

I clutched the bottle of wine that I'd brought as a hostess gift and took a calming breath as I climbed out of the car. Luna bounced out and hustled me toward the front door, which was ajar.

"We'll go right on in then," said Luna beaming as she pushed the door further open. I shut it on the other side and followed Luna into the brightly-lit space.

It was just as beautiful on the inside as it had been on the outside. Grace had opted for lots of wooden furniture mixed with warm-colored fabrics. And I was pleased to see there were bookshelves everywhere. Naturally, I thought books made for the perfect décor.

A woman in her late-thirties wearing an elegant caftan sort of coverup came toward us. Luna gave her an enthusiastic hug and then introduced me. "Grace, this is Ann. Ann, Grace."

Grace gave me a two-handed handshake and said warmly, "Hi, Ann. I'm so glad you could make it out this weekend."

The last lingering feelings of possibly intruding on the group quickly disappeared and I gave a sigh of relief. Grace was clearly completely genuine about her welcome.

"I'm happy to be here," I said, feeling pretty genuine myself. "You have a beautiful home."

She beamed at me and glanced around. "Thank you. I'm finally really happy with the way it turned out. But I promised myself I'd never have another house built as long as I lived! I knew on one level that it would mean a lot of decisions. But I don't think I really *realized* exactly how many decisions it would take. I mean, even trying to decide between a hundred different faucets. I'm just relieved it didn't end up being a total disaster."

I said, "You must have really good instincts."

Grace laughed. "No, I think I just had a really good designer. She made sure to show me only options that *would* work. But it was still a lot of options. Come on in and I'll get you a drink and introduce you to everybody else."

Luna said, "Everybody sure got here super-early. We're right on time." She's pretty sensitive about being on time because it used to be a thing at the library where Wilson noticed she was coming in a few minutes tardy each day. His displeasure had definitely made her more punctual.

Grace grinned at her. "I guess everyone wanted to start their weekend earlier."

We followed her into a tremendous kitchen with several eating areas which somehow managed to retain the cabin-like feel of the house while having all the latest gadgets. She walked up to a large island in the center of the space where she'd set up a makeshift bar.

Grace said ruefully, "I hope you won't think badly of us that we've started drinking. In our defense the drinks are bloody Marys and mimosas."

"Totally respectable drinks for the morning," agreed Luna stoutly.

Grace added, "We also have soft drinks, ice tea, and water. So whatever you feel like. I thought we'd go out on the boat in a few minutes since everyone's here. I had my favorite deli cater a brunch for us and I thought it might be fun if we had it out on the boat."

"That sounds amazing," I said with a smile. And it did. It beat weeding books out of the library collection, which is what I'd have been doing if I was at work.

Luna went boldly for a bloody Mary. I wasn't sure exactly how much alcohol was in the bloody Marys or the mimosas, so I decided to pour myself a small glass of white wine. A little bit of Dutch courage would be good for me, and at least I'd know exactly how much alcohol I was consuming.

We followed Grace into a huge living room with vaulted ceilings. There was a massive stone fireplace at one end. The furniture looked cushy and comfortable and one piece likely cost more than most of my den furniture put together. There were five or six men and women in there and they called out a greeting as we came closer.

"Okay, ready for the introductions?" asked Grace.

"I'll quiz you later," said Roz mischievously.

A handsome man in his late-30s waved at me. "Let intro-duce ourselves," he said. "I always think it's easier to remember that way than with someone pointing and giving a whole bunch of names at once. I'm Scott Haynsworth."

The blonde woman next to him grinned. "And I'm Kelly, Scott's girlfriend."

A serious-looking man wearing black framed glasses looked around and then spoke. "Kyle Hubbard." He hesitated. "Good to meet you."

"And lastly, Felicity Patton," said a thin woman with long, dark hair.

Grace clasped her hands together. "Not that little administrative task is done, let's head out on the boat."

Kelly asked, "Is it going to be warm out there? Or should I bring a sweater with me?"

"I'll keep you warm," said Scott with a wink, gallantly putting his arm around her.

I noticed that Kyle only seemed to have eyes for Felicity. When she glanced his way, though, he looked flustered and turned away.

We all helped Grace carry the coolers and assorted food containers out of the house and down a brick pathway to the boat. Somehow, in my mind, I'd been expecting a run-of-the-mill pontoon boat. This boat was anything but, and I wasn't sure why I'd been thinking a pontoon would go with the property it belonged to. This wasn't a boat . . . it was a yacht. It had an enclosed downstairs and an upper deck that was open. It looked like a house on the water. Luna and I exchanged a quick look.

Grace saw the look and said, "Don't worry, I don't usually have a boat like this here. It would be *way* too big for just me. In the dock is a ski boat and another boat. I rented this one for the weekend. It even came with a captain."

Sure enough, I saw there was a man wearing a captain's hat ready to assist everyone getting on the boat. I thought that was overkill until I noticed some of the party actually seemed to have already had a couple of drinks and were a little unsteady on their feet. He also helped get the coolers and food on the boat.

"Music, I think," said Grace with a grin. "I got a preview of where everything was earlier." She took out her phone, which had already been synched with the ship's stereo system and soon classic rock was playing through the speakers.

"Alcohol, I think," said Scott with a wink. "I'll play bartender."

I noticed that the captain's brow crinkled and he studied Scott with a frown for a moment before leaving to start piloting the boat.

Scott created a bar on one of the tables scattered across the bottom level of the boat.

Grace said, "We should probably have some drinks upstairs, too, since that's where most of us will probably end up hanging out."

Felicity asked, "It won't be cold up there?"

"Maybe on the way out. But the captain is going to put down an anchor at a scenic part of the lake and we'll be there for a while to enjoy the view and eat and all. It shouldn't be cold then," said Grace.

We stayed on the bottom level while the boat made its way out. Luna and I helped Grace unpack the food. There was a *lot* of food and it looked delicious. There were containers of every kind of sandwich spread imaginable: chicken salad, tuna salad, a veggie spread, egg salad, deli hams and turkeys and sliced turkeys and fancy mustards and mayos to go with them. The bread was fresh and clearly from a bakery and there were all different types. She'd also brought in all various fruits and chips and sides to go along with them. It was enough food to feed an army and I wasn't at all sure I would be hungry for supper.

Grace said, "Let's help our plates. Somebody has to go first."

There was a moment of hesitation as there so frequently is when it's time for people to start eating and nobody wanted to look greedy or pushy. Scott said, "Oh, come on people. I'll go first, okay. But someone has to go second."

"Me!" said Luna enthusiastically.

Scott strode over and fixed himself a couple of sandwiches and loaded his plate with potato salad and deviled eggs with Luna right behind him. After that, everyone followed suit and soon the atmosphere was more relaxed.

I sat down next to Luna and she smiled at me. "So, what do you think so far? This boat is crazy, isn't it?"

I nodded, mouth full of sandwich. I had the feeling that it wasn't just the *boat* that was crazy.

Luna followed my gaze and chuckled as Scott gulped down a shot of vodka and whooped loudly. "Yeah, I agree with you. Scott's a little crazy, too."

"What do you know about him?" I asked after taking a sip of water.

She shrugged. "I know him a little, like I know them all a little. Roz has talked about them through the years and I guess that makes me feel like I know them better than I do. I'm older than everybody, of course."

Chapter Three

Scott did seem to be flirting with Felicity, who didn't seem particularly receptive. Or maybe she *would* have been receptive if Scott's girlfriend hadn't been shooting them daggers with her eyes. Scott seemed totally oblivious to this fact. Kelly, in turn, struck up a conversation with Kyle, who was miserably watching Scott and Felicity together.

"Looks like a set-up for drama," drawled Luna. "And Grace doesn't look too pleased, either."

Sure enough, Grace's eyes were cold as she looked at Scott, then became shuttered.

Luna said, "I'm just glad Grace brought some vegan options. I mean, that was super-sweet, wasn't it? She'd sent out an email to see what kind of food preferences and allergies and stuff that people had. What a thoughtful hostess."

Roz plopped down next to them and heard the last bit of what Luna said. "If only she hadn't invited Scott, then it would be the perfect day." She rolled her eyes.

"Yeah, what is *up* with him?" asked Luna. "The times I've met him, he's been a *little* obnoxious, but never *that* obnoxious. He needs to stop flirting with Felicity."

"Who knows? I guess it's the alcohol, although he should be used to it. He's not exactly a teetotaler. Anyway, the booze isn't helping," said Roz. "I wish those two would just break up."

Luna peered across at Scott and Felicity. Felicity seemed to be trying to make distance between her and Scott, although she was still diffidently engaging in conversation with him. Scott appeared to be talking a real blue streak, in comparison. Luna said dryly, "Well, you might get your wish, Roz. Kelly sure doesn't seem happy about Scott chatting up Felicity."

Roz said, "I know I'm a mean friend, but it's the best thing that could happen to Kelly. She wastes so much energy trying to make that relationship work when anyone can see it's doomed. There's so much else she could do with her time if she didn't have to worry about Scott."

Roz stopped talking abruptly as Grace came up. "The captain is throwing down the anchor. Want to head upstairs and hang out for a while?"

"Absolutely," said Luna, beaming. "Can't wait."

"Who wants a frosé?" asked Kelly.

There were a lot of enthusiastic affirmations. I hated to sound like the rube in the group, but I had to ask, "What's a frosé?"

"it's wonderful," said Grace. "You'll want one."

I felt a little dubious on that point.

Luna said, "It's a frozen rosé with sugar and strawberry syrup added to it. Really good, especially when it's a warm day."

And it was. It felt light and refreshing when she poured one for me, although I knew I was going to have to counter it with some water at some point.

The top deck was warm and the sun felt fantastic. I could feel my spirits lifting. There were comfy chaise-lounges everywhere with pillows and fluffy towels. Scott had brought drinks up to accompany the frosés (mostly beer) and Grace had light snacks and water upstairs. The view was spectacular. The leaves were at their peak and sported bright yellows, rich reds, and golden-oranges. The mountains seemed to spring up from the lake. For the first time since arriving, I actually relaxed.

Grace changed the station on her phone and the music was more low-key with acoustic songs and softer folk music. Everyone was chatting together for the first few minutes. Kyle came to sit next to me and ask me about work. It was a subject I could warm to, although I had to always be careful not to go on and on about it until I sounded like an advertisement for the Whitby Library. But Kyle was interested in the programs and I was happy to talk about them.

"That's really cool," he said finally. "I'm over there a lot, but I'm usually just running in to pick up a book and then running back out again. I remember seeing you over there, though."

"I remember you, too," I said. "What is it you mostly like to read?"

We talked a few more minutes together, although I could see his attention wavering sometimes and his gaze was pulled over to where Felicity was sitting. Scott was no longer sitting next to her, but he was still trying to engage her in conversation from a couple of seats away. Grace gave us a thoughtful look and smiled when she saw me glance her way.

Kyle moved on to speak with Grace and Luna plopped down next to me.

"I want a nap," she said in a drowsy voice. "And it's still early afternoon."

"It's probably the food," I said. "We all ate plenty of it."

Luna snorted. "It's probably the alcohol. Maybe the food a *little* bit."

A few minutes later, she was sound asleep, mouth slightly agape as the conversation continued in the background.

Scott said, "I'm going to swim. Anybody want to go with me?"

Kyle shook his head and said a little stiffly, "I didn't bring a suit."

"You didn't put one on under your clothes? We're on a boat, man! You didn't think about going swimming?"

"Not when it's this chilly," said Kyle in a slightly disapproving tone.

Grace said, "I think you're going to be on your own, Scott. But the captain pointed out there was some sort of diving board on the bottom level."

He quirked an eyebrow. "Not on the top level? How disappointing."

Roz said sharply, "I guess he didn't want the liability if someone broke his neck."

Scott scoffed. "It's just a swim, guys. See you in a few."

He took off his shirt and headed down the stairs to the lower level of the boat.

Kelly said, "This, I've got to see. He's probably going to turn blue. Want to come with me, Kyle?" They followed Scott downstairs.

Roz looked at Grace. "Scott's being *so* obnoxious today. Even worse than usual. He's really baiting Kelly. And drinking way too much."

Grace sighed. "I know. Let's try to view his antics as entertainment for the group."

Felicity said, "I don't see it as being very entertaining."

"No, of course you don't," said Grace. "If you want me to, I can call him a taxi and ask him to leave. I only invited him here because he was part of our old group at school and because he's dating Kelly. His drinking must have gotten a lot worse than I remember it being."

Felicity shook her head. "No, I don't want that. He's just really irritating, that's all, especially with Kelly right there."

Roz said darkly, "Yeah, Kelly isn't appreciating it, but she knows it's not your fault, Felicity. I'd like to give Scott a piece of my mind. It's too bad this boat is so tidy. I remember that Scott's terrified of bugs. *That* might be entertaining."

Felicity said, "I'm going to make myself a lemonade. A little hydration is in order. Anybody want to join me?"

"Good idea. I'll come along," said Roz.

"I think I'm going to follow Luna's lead and doze off for a little while," said Grace with a chuckle.

"And I think I'm halfway there," I said sleepily, surprising myself. I wasn't usually one for taking naps, but the lulling motion of the boat and the food and drink I'd had weren't helping. I slid on my sunglasses, pushed the chaise all the way back and fell into a gentle sleep.

I wasn't sure how much time had passed when I woke up to what sounded like an angry, hushed conversation. The nice thing about my sunglasses were that they were mirrored and totally opaque. I opened my eyes to see who was talking.

It was Scott and Grace and whatever they were talking about, neither one looked very happy. Scott was sneering and swaggering—or possibly staggering—as he weaved in front of Grace. Grace was still seated and looked coldly furious. No one else was on the upper deck besides me and Luna, snoring away beside me.

Scott said, "You're wrong if you think I won't go through with it, Grace."

"Friendship clearly counts for nothing, does it?" Grace asked briskly.

"Friendship? There are friends and there are friends. I'm not going to let a childhood friendship from ages ago affect what I do today. Besides, it's hard to be friends with someone like you," said Scott.

"Keep quiet!" she hissed. Grace looked right at me and I froze, feeling like she could somehow tell I was awake.

He laughed. "You're worried about those two? They're total lightweights, Grace. They're out cold. The two librarians aren't used to drinking that much."

"Look, you'll get it," said Grace in a clipped voice.

"Just make sure I do. I'm glad Kelly got you to invite me. Aren't we having fun? Now I'm going to head downstairs to get a real drink . . . there's only beer left up here."

I saw him head to the stairs, unsteady on his feet. Grace stayed behind and took deep breaths as if to collect herself. She stood up and held onto the rail tightly, staring off blankly at the gorgeous view for a few minutes before slowly heading downstairs, herself.

I was glad I was finally able to move because I was starting to get a real crick in my neck, but hadn't wanted to disturb the conversation. I glanced over at Luna and saw she was turning a really unhealthy shade of red.

"Hey, Luna," I said softly. She snored on and I reached out a hand and gently touched her arm. "Hey, you need to wake up."

"What for?" asked Luna groggily. She frowned and sat up, as if realizing where she was. "Wow, I was really out."

"I know. I took a nap, too. It must be all the sun and food. But you're starting to burn."

"What?" asked Luna again. She took her sunglasses off and studied her skin, gingerly touching it. She grimaced. "Great. Yeah, I'm burned, all right. This is going to feel awful tomorrow."

"Want to borrow some sunscreen?" I asked.

"It's a little late for that," said Luna wryly. "I probably should just stay out of the sun for the rest of the day." She glanced around. "Where did everybody go?"

"They're all downstairs. I'm pretty sure the boat is going to start heading back to the house in a few minutes." I added in a low voice, "While you were sleeping, I overheard a really weird conversation between Scott and Grace."

Luna's eyebrows flew up. "Really? Tell me about it?"

"I don't know exactly what I was hearing because I woke up in the middle of it. But it almost sounded like Scott was trying to force Grace into something. He said he'd definitely *go through with it* and then she said she'd *make sure he got it.* I don't know what they were talking about, but it wasn't friendly."

Luna blinked. "Huh. That's weird. They were good friends when they were in school. Let's go downstairs and see what's going on now. If he's had even more booze, there's no telling what we might see or hear."

But when we got back downstairs, everything seemed to be normal. Kelly and Scott were sitting together and Scott was actually being attentive, getting up to refresh her drink or to get Kelly a snack. Kyle was tentatively having a conversation with Felicity, who was smiling at him. And Grace and Roz were chatting together.

The boat started moving again to head back to the house. Roz glanced over at us and her eyes grew big. "Wow, Luna, you're burned to a crisp!"

Grace made a face. "That's got to hurt."

Luna said sadly, "Not yet, but I'm sure it will soon."

"I have aloe vera back at the house," said Grace.

"Good. I'm going to slather it all over myself," said Luna glumly. "I can't believe I forgot to put sunscreen on. But now that it's fall and with the air as cool as it was, I guess I just didn't think about it."

"Aloe vera, for sure. And maybe take an ibuprofen, too," said Roz, wincing. Then she asked, "So what's the plan for the rest of the day?"

Grace said, "I wanted to make sure I didn't overschedule everybody, so I built in some downtime this afternoon. When we get back, everybody can take a nap, or play ping pong or pool, take a swim in the pool, or go for a walk. There's an amazing trail that the neighborhood association keeps up, if anyone is looking for exercise. Then I thought we'd have supper on the screen porch."

I'd glimpsed the screen porch earlier and it definitely wasn't a modest or casual space. It was more like a tremendous room with a carpet, a television, a stone fireplace, fancy ceiling fans, what appeared to be stained mahogany floors, and wooden chairs and sofas with cushy linen pillows and cushions.

I said, "I can help you put supper together, Grace."

She gave me a smile. "Thanks for that. I really appreciate the offer, but I'm having it catered and there's a team to serve it and to clean up."

Luna shook her head. "You've put a lot of time and thought into this weekend. And . . . money."

Grace said, "It's really nothing—I've really looked forward to having a party like this. It's been sort of a stressful year and this is one way for me to see friends, get to make some new friends, and bless my new house. I'm just delighted to have everybody here."

When we got back to the house, everyone went their separate ways. Luna followed Grace in to get some aloe vera and have a nap. Felicity declared she needed to stretch her legs a little and Kyle quickly said he'd join her for a walk on the trail that Grace had pointed out. Roz said she'd swim some laps in the pool. And I climbed into the hammock with my book in a section of Grace's wooded yard facing the lake. I gave a deep, happy sigh. The hammock was almost like being in a bed—it actually had a thin mattress covering it and a soft pillow. Even though I'd fallen asleep on the boat, this was the point where I felt completely relaxed. I could hear the water lapping gently against the dock, birds singing as they visited the nearby bird feeders. And the trees above me provided shade from the bright sunshine.

The backyard itself was amazing, aside from the lake. It had been landscaped with mature bushes providing nooks with benches and comfortable chairs to relax in. It all lent a beautiful, private air to the space.

I started reading *And Then There Were None* again, marveling over the way Agatha Christie had created such a mysterious atmosphere at the isolated island party in the story. A few pages in, I heard voices approaching. They settled in one of the garden nooks nearby and I grimaced. It looked like I was going to be eavesdropping again. The voices, which I recognized as Scott's and Kelly's, were already engaged in an argument, so I didn't want to make myself known . . . they'd likely already be embarrassed.

"Slow down with the drinking," said Kelly in a furious voice. "It's like you're on a mission to get sloppy drunk. I don't understand—you're not always like this."

"Maybe I just need a break," snapped Scott in a slurred voice. "Don't you ever take a break?"

"Not like this. You're starting to humiliate yourself."

Scott drawled, "Funny, I don't *feel* humiliated."

"Well, you should. You've been rude to everybody. What you should be doing right now is going off to take a nap. Take a break from the booze. Then you can start up again at dinner if you want to. But if you keep hitting the bottle as hard as you have been, you're going to make a total fool of yourself."

Scott said in a sarcastic tone, "I do appreciate your concern, Kelly. But I'm totally fine. Look, I've been under a ton of stress lately. Is it so bad that I'm taking the chance to unwind at an absolutely gorgeous lake house in the mountains? Nobody else seems as uptight about my drinking as you are."

"That's because they're trying to be polite," hissed Kelly. "I bet there's one person who wants you to stop drinking. Felicity. You need to just back off."

"I haven't *done* anything. I'm just being friendly. Besides, I have something I need to talk to her about. These are people we haven't seen in ages—it's good to just catch up with them."

Kelly said, "I think there's more going on here than just catching up."

I heard sound of sticks and leaves underfoot as Kelly left. "Oh, come on, Kelly. Don't be like that," called Scott after her. Then he gave a dramatic sigh and followed her.

Chapter Four

After that, it was blessedly quiet. I had gotten my fill of quarreling guests and happily delved back into the wonderful, deadly, world of Agatha Christie until it was time to get ready for dinner.

Since dinner had sounded like a pretty fancy affair, I put on my black dress and some simple jewelry and headed back downstairs to join the others. I was relieved to hear the sound of laughter when I walked out on the porch. Apparently, everyone had lightened up and was prepared to be on their best behavior for the dinner that Grace had clearly put some effort into planning. Even Scott appeared to be behaving himself.

The porch was lit up with candles as the sun set and the table was laden with food—side dishes of every type imaginable. There were servers hovering in the wings, waiting for us all to settle before the main course was brought out. We all sat down where our place cards told us to go and Grace started us off with a toast. "To friendship," she said with a warm smile to everyone as we all took a sip of our champagne.

Grace added, "We have a variety of food here, hopefully something for everyone. For the meat lovers, the main course is a London broil with herb butter. For the vegetarians among us, there are grilled bruschetta portobello mushrooms and eggplant cannelloni. There should be enough of everything for the London broil folks to have both."

I said genuinely, "Grace, this is fantastic. Thanks so much."

She waved her hand, dismissing my compliment with a smile. "It's my pleasure. I was so looking forward to this and had fun figuring out the menu."

The servers quickly came around, dipping in front of us as they proffered various dishes for us to help ourselves from. The food was melt-in-your-mouth good and the view was just as fabulous as the sun set behind the mountains, creating a color palette that rivaled the changing leaves and reflected pinks and purples on the still water of the lake.

Luna, next to me, gave a contented sigh. "I could get used to this."

I grinned at her. "We might have chosen the wrong profession if we're aspiring to this lifestyle."

"Totally," said Luna with a snort. "It's just a good thing I like books more than I like . . . all this." She gave a wave of her hand to encompass everything around her.

Felicity was on my other side and struck up a polite conversation with me about the library.

"I hate to admit it, but I haven't been much of a reader." She grimaced. "I feel like it makes me sound stupid to say it. But in the last few years, whenever I've tried to pick up a novel, I just couldn't focus on it. I kept feeling like there was something else I needed to be doing. I'd end up reading the same paragraph over and over again before I just totally gave up and went back to my spreadsheets."

I said, "Were you only trying to read fiction, then?" She nodded her head and I added, "You might find it easier to read nonfiction, instead. There are a lot that are very popular with our readers who are big in business that you might enjoy. *Lean In* by Sheryl Sandberg is one that a lot of businesswomen have enjoyed."

Felicity brightened at this. "I didn't even think about that. The people I've spoken with, whenever they recommend a book, they're always talking about fiction bestsellers."

"Nonfiction might be a better match for you right now," I said. "I could email you some recommendations, if you'd like."

She immediately fished out her phone and sent me her contact information via text.

I said, "We also have a book club at the library that focuses a lot on nonfiction."

"Could you send me the info on that, too?" asked Felicity.

Roz grinned down the table. "I hear Ann talking about work. Remember, we're supposed to be taking a break here."

Kelly snorted. "As if you take many breaks, yourself, Roz. You know you love your job just as much as Ann does."

"And me!" piped up Luna, raising a hand.

"What is it that you do, Roz?" I asked. I felt like she or Luna had told me at some point but I couldn't remember.

"I'm a nurse," said Roz. "And Kelly's right—I love it. The patients are usually great and I like that I'm helping people."

Kelly said, "What *I* couldn't handle about your job—well, actually, there are *plenty* of things I couldn't handle—is the shift you work. I'd never be able to function. And here you are during normal hours and you seem perfectly fine."

"I've just gotten used to it." She glanced around and filled everyone in. "It's a 3 a.m. to 3 p.m. shift, but it's only for three days in a row and then I get four days off. It's easier to adjust to it that way."

Everyone continued with pleasant conversation and eating until finally we'd all reached a stopping point.

Luna said, "That was so good, but if I keep eating, someone is going to have to roll me away from the table."

Grace said, "Is anyone up for a swim? It might be a good way to work off some of the food we just ate. And I like to have a little exercise in the evenings."

"Won't it be too chilly to swim?" asked Kyle, raising an eyebrow.

"The pool is actually indoors," said Grace. "And we can bring our drinks with us. It should be really relaxing."

Everyone agreed and went up to change clothes. Fifteen minutes later, we were all gathered around the pool. The pool room was just as elegant as the screen porch had been. One of the walls was stone, the ceiling and other three walls were glass so, as you swam, you could look up at the moon and stars or across to the mountains and lake. There was a cabinet full of soft, thick towels and white robes in the corner of the large room. And there was a full bar with champagne bottles in ice waiting for them.

Luna leaned over and said to me, "I don't know about you, but I'm way too full to exercise right now."

"I'm the same way. I couldn't seem to stop filling my plate," I said wryly. "Do you want to exercise first thing tomorrow, instead? That's usually a better time for me, anyway."

Luna nodded. "Before everyone gets up? Maybe six or six-thirty?"

Grace overheard what we were saying and nodded. "The pool temperature is always set really warm, too, so it won't be a shock to your system going in that early. Or, if it is, you can always warm up over there." She pointed to a hot tub, which I hadn't even noticed when I came in.

Luna grinned. "I may not be able to exercise now, but sitting in a hot tub sounds right up my alley."

"Mine, too," chimed in Roz and the three of us made our way over to the large tub. Grace hit a couple of buttons and the hot tub's lights came on and the water bubbled up.

"Once again," breathed Luna, "I could get used to this."

The three of us chatted a little, but were mostly just enjoying the warm water, which was working wonders on my tight muscles. When the jets, which were on a timer, cut off, I could hear the unwelcome sounds of nearby quarreling. I glanced over and saw Scott and Kelly engaged in another heated argument at the side of the pool.

Roz groaned. "I think I'm ready for those jets to turn on again. What's Scott done this time?"

Luna shrugged. "I didn't see it. Guessing it's the same thing. Scott's drinking too much and being obnoxious."

This time, though, whatever Scott had said or done seemed to have a 'final straw' aspect about it.

"I'm getting out of here," said Kelly. "I'm not going to subject myself or the rest of the group to this anymore."

Grace shook her head. "Please stay put, Kelly. You shouldn't be driving a car. None of us should."

"Who said I was going to drive?" demanded Kelly, giving Grace an impatient look. "I'm walking. Anybody want to come? There's a band playing at the club. It's just a short walk. Live music, booze, and lakefront views."

"I'll go," said Roz quickly.

"Sorry, I think I'm starting to wind down," Felicity demurred. The rest of us shook our heads.

Scott snorted and Kelly rolled her eyes. She and Roz left on foot around the side of the house toward the road.

Scott was acting as if he couldn't possibly care less that Kelly was leaving. "Now the party can *really* kick off," he said with a lopsided grin.

Felicity stood up and said, "Sorry, but I'm going to bow out. Maybe I had too much sun today, but I'm exhausted. I'm going to head upstairs and turn in early. Thanks for everything, Grace." She turned and left.

The sudden disappearance of nearly everyone in the party was starting to resemble the Agatha Christie I was reading. And then there were none, for sure.

Scott looked over at Kyle, who'd been quietly watching everything unfold. He said in a mocking tone, "You look so disapproving, Kyle. What's wrong?"

Kyle said coldly, "You know what's wrong. You're being rude and thoughtless to the other guests and to Grace, who's set all this up."

Scott turned and looked pointedly at Grace. "Grace isn't exactly the paragon of virtue she appears to be. Are you, Grace?"

Grace's expression was icy as she stared at Scott.

Scott gave a short laugh. "Besides, it takes two to argue. Why isn't anybody complaining about Kelly?"

"Because you're the one instigating the arguments," said Kyle.

Scott shrugged. "Time to go for a swim. Maybe the rest of you should do the same and give yourselves a chance to cool off." He dove into the water and started swimming laps.

Grace gave me an apologetic look. "Ann, I'm so sorry. You came here to relax for the weekend and it's been pretty stressful."

I shook my head. "No, I've really enjoyed myself. It's beautiful out here. And you don't have anything to apologize for—you can't control what your guests do."

"If only she could," said Kyle glumly.

Grace smiled at me. "I really appreciate it, Ann."

Although I was dying to retreat upstairs myself, I felt like I shouldn't desert Grace yet. She *had* put a lot of time into this party and I didn't want to just abandon her. So Luna and I hung out for an hour or more—listening to music, reading, and hanging out with everyone.

Then we heard the front door through the open pool door. "Kelly? Roz?" Grace called out.

Roz came toward us with a sheepish smile. "Just Roz. Kelly was . . . overserved at the club. I just dropped her off back home."

Scott gave a dark chuckle and Roz gave him a cold look. She pressed her lips tightly closed as if forcing words back.

Scott, however, didn't seem quite as prudent. "Still trying to protect her, Roz? I don't think anybody else thinks I'm so awful." He hiccupped at this and weaved unsteadily at the side of the pool.

"Yeah, because you're such a catch. Forgetting birthdays, picking fights." Roz shrugged. She headed to the bar next to the pool and poured herself a large glass of champagne which she drank quickly.

Luna raised her eyebrows as Roz poured herself another glass and quickly dispatched it. It made me wince. Champagne hits the bloodstream fast because of the bubbles. And the only hangover I've ever had was from a very small amount of it.

Roz continued, "All the two of you do is torture each other. You need to break it off. I keep telling Kelly that, but she won't listen, so maybe you need to be the one to do it. You're making each other totally miserable and that kind of stress can't be good for your health."

"Says Nurse Nancy," drawled Scott. He poured himself another drink of champagne. "I'll just have to drown my sorrows. Alcohol is good for relieving stress, too."

Roz shook her head. "I'm sorry, Grace, but I'm heading upstairs, too. I've got a splitting headache. Brought on by you-know-who."

Grace frowned. "Can I get you some ibuprofen or an aspirin?"

"Thanks, but I brought some with me. I thought I might have a hangover." She gave a short laugh. "It's more of a Scott-induced migraine. I'll be fine, though."

I said, "Just the same, though, it's been a really full day. I think I might turn in early. Luna and I are talking about having an early-morning swim and I'll sleep through my alarm if I don't get to bed."

Luna quickly added, "Me, too. But it's been fun today, Grace, really. We appreciate the invitation."

Kyle said, "I'm going to hang out for a while down here and catch up with Grace. After I grab myself a beer."

"There's champagne over there," said Grace.

Kyle grimaced. "I think I'd better stick with something weaker, but thanks."

Luna and I gathered our stuff together and headed upstairs.

Luna said in a library whisper, "This party has gotten weird. I've never seen Scott like this before. Usually he's pretty easy-going and fun to be with."

"That's hard to imagine right now," I said dryly.

"Anyway, it was nice of you to make Grace feel better. I feel bad she's put a lot of time and money into this party and Scott seems determined to ruin it."

I stopped in front of my room and said, "He can't do that. Besides, he might be fine now that Kelly has left. Most of the conflict was between those two, after all. He's got to be better tomorrow morning, anyway, after he's had a good night's sleep and before he starts drinking for the day. Tomorrow will probably be much smoother."

"You're setting your alarm for tomorrow?" asked Luna.

"I've already set it. I'll meet you at the pool," I said.

After I'd undressed and gotten ready for bed, I could still hear voices and someone had turned on some music. Maybe Roz or Felicity had gone back to the pool. I pulled out the pair of earplugs I always travel with and plugged up my ears. With all the sounds silenced, I quickly fell into a deep sleep until my alarm went off the next morning.

I got up and put on my suit, then headed downstairs to the pool. Luna hadn't made it down yet, apparently, so I did a few light stretches in preparation for the swim.

Then I decided to go ahead and get in the pool and get adjusted to the water temperature, although Grace had assured us it would feel warm. As I walked to the edge of the pool, my blood suddenly ran cold as I saw a body floating face-down in the water.

Chapter Six

I grabbed a life preserver ring from a hook on the wall and jumped into the pool with it, swimming over to the body. I flipped the body over and saw it was Scott Haynsworth. I treaded water as I held onto both the life preserver and Scott and then swam for the side of the pool. I heard Luna yell out to me and run over to the side of the pool.

"Help me get him out," I said, gasping. I shoved Scott up from the water and Luna reached down and pulled him out at the same time.

"Is he dead?" asked Luna shakily.

"Don't know. Run get some help," I said, still breathless.

I tried to shake Scott awake, saying his name loudly but there was no response. I also saw his head was bloodied. I tilted his head to the side for any water to drain away, then I turned it to the center. I tried to clear his airway, laying him on his back and tilting his chin and head back. I looked at his chest as I put my head close to his mouth to feel or hear breathing, but there was nothing.

Luna came back with some of the others and I started mouth-to-mouth resuscitation and chest compressions. After a minute, I tried to feel for a pulse and felt nothing.

Grace took over at this point, then Kyle, but there were no results.

"I think he's gone," I said quietly.

Grace, who'd been hovering nearby, sat back on her heels with a defeated expression. "I called 911," she said dully. "They should be here any moment."

I started shivering uncontrollably and Kyle strode to the cabinet in the corner and pulled out towels and one of the robes for me.

Grace said softly, "What happened, Ann?"

I said, "I was meeting Luna for our morning swim. I stretched for a few minutes because I was the first one downstairs."

Luna winced. "It took me longer to get ready this morning."

"Then I thought I'd go ahead and get into the pool and get adjusted to the water temperature. That's when I saw Scott." Finally, my shivering had eased up and my teeth had stopped chattering.

Kyle asked, "He was floating in the pool?"

I nodded. "Face-down."

Everyone was quiet for a few moments after hearing this. Scott could have been in the pool most of the night. Who knew how long he'd been floating like that?

"What happened to his head?" asked Kyle, his voice sounding a little strangled.

Luna said, "It looks like he was hit on the head."

Kyle pointed to a bottle of champagne that was lying on its side. "With that?"

It sure looked like it. This plunged us back into silence as everyone tried to absorb the impact of Scott's injury.

We heard sirens approaching and Grace stood up. "I'll greet them out front."

The EMTs came in first, hurrying over to Scott. After several minutes, it was clear to them that nothing could be done.

A couple of minutes later, Burton walked into the pool room. I relaxed when I saw him. He had a very solid, comforting presence. He was a big guy with a receding hairline, a steady gaze, and currently a very concerned expression. One of the EMTs spoke with him for a moment and he nodded and then turned to the rest of us.

"Hey, everybody," he said firmly. "I know this has been a shock. But I need you all to move out of this room. I passed through a living room on the way in—maybe wait for me in there?"

We all numbly nodded and silently filed out. Grace led us into the big living room and turned on the gas fire since my shivering started up again despite the warmth of the fluffy towel. She walked to the kitchen and returned with a pot of coffee and a tray of cups, sugar, and cream.

Twenty minutes later, more police officers arrived and a few guys in forensics suits. Burton must have made phone calls to the state police, as well.

Grace gazed blankly at the different authorities as they walked by. "I can't believe this is happening," she murmured.

Roz reached over and gave her a hug. "He probably just hit his head on the side of the pool when he went in."

Grace shook her head. "How would he have been able to do that? Going in head-first?"

"He was doing some shallow diving for a while," said Roz.

I agreed with Grace. From the spot on his head, I couldn't figure how he'd have gotten that injury in a natural way. It was on the back of his head. Unless Scott was trying to attempt a back dive, there was just no way he could have gotten that cut. And there wasn't a diving board.

Kyle said in a low voice, "They're going to ask us questions. They'll think one of us was involved."

That seemed very likely. We were all silent again. I could definitely see how someone in our group might have wanted to permanently get rid of Scott. He'd behaved badly the entire time he'd been here and had had spats with nearly everyone.

Roz was still determined to believe it had all been an accident of some kind. "Maybe not. After all, he was drinking a lot. I mean a *lot*. He could have staggered around the pool and slipped or something, like I said. Let's wait and see what happens."

We were all quiet again. Then I said, "Shouldn't someone tell Kelly?"

Grace and Roz froze and then looked at each other.

Roz said, "This is going to kill her, especially how they ended things. Maybe we should let her just sleep."

Grace shook her head. "Ann is right. Kelly should know. I don't think she'd thank us for keeping her in the dark about Scott's death."

Roz shook her head and then winced as if her head hurt.

"I'll do it," said Grace quietly.

I was glad someone did because I had the feeling if the police were going to be questioning us, they were definitely going to want to talk to Kelly. She knew Scott better than anyone—and she'd been arguing with him before his death.

Burton joined us again, looking grim. "Sorry for the wait, guys. I know this must be a huge shock for you. We are going to need to take statements from everybody. He looked at Grace. "Is this your home?"

She nodded, looking pale.

"Is there a quiet spot where we can speak separately with everyone here?" asked Burton.

She nodded again and stood up, looking a little shaky on her feet. "My study is right off of this room. Will that work?" She led him over to it and Burton pulled another chair inside.

He looked over at me. "Ann, could I speak with you first?"

I followed him to the study, which looked more like a mini-library. There were books lining the walls from floor to ceiling. Ordinarily, my first instinct would have been to peruse the shelves. Grace had a mahogany desk in the space and a Persian rug. I sat down in a leather armchair.

Burton sighed. "So what's going on here? Can you sketch it all out for me so I have some direction with my questions with everyone? What's the set-up?"

"Grace Armstrong, who just helped you set up the room, is the hostess. This is a sort of housewarming party for her . . . she wanted to introduce friends to her new home and relax."

Burton nodded. "And you're friends with her."

I shook my head. "Actually, I just met her. She was open to meeting new people and wanted Luna to have someone to hang out with, I think."

Burton frowned. "So Luna is friends with Grace."

"I wouldn't say they were the type of friends who actually hung out together. Luna knows Grace from when she grew up here. Luna's here mainly because her cousin Roz is friends with Grace and the rest of the guests."

Burton started taking notes.

I continued. "So the rest of the guests knew each other when they were in school together. It sounds like they were pretty close back then, but Grace moved away and just recently came back to Whitby."

"With a good deal of money," muttered Burton with a glance around the well-appointed study. "And the victim?"

"*Is* he a victim, then? He was definitely murdered? We wondered if maybe he'd tried diving in and hit his head, was knocked unconscious, and then drowned."

Burton shook his head. "That explanation could have worked if we hadn't spotted the bloody champagne bottle. Sadly, someone thought to wipe it clean of fingerprints."

I stared at him. "So he *was* murdered, then."

"Any ideas why?"

I nodded slowly. "His name is Scott Haynsworth. Unfortunately, he was a pretty difficult guest this weekend."

"In what way?"

"First off, he and his girlfriend were squabbling the whole time. Her name is Kelly and she left the party last night because she'd had enough. Scott was drinking too much and generally being obnoxious. Running his mouth and flirting with someone else," I said.

Burton's brows knit together. "Flirting with who?"

I almost smiled, but carefully kept my mouth from turning up at the corners. I knew Burton had a warm spot for Luna, although he never seemed to be able to make too much progress with her and she appeared to have no idea that he was interested in her at all.

"Felicity. I think her name is Felicity Patton. She works at one of the big banks."

"In Whitby?" Burton's eyebrows flew up his wide forehead.

"No, she works remotely and flies a lot."

Burton carefully added more notes to his notebook. "And was she receptive to his flirting?"

"Not at all. She was basically avoiding him the whole time. But then, she's also friends with Kelly and wouldn't have wanted to make her upset," I said.

"Who else was he at odds with?"

I thought about this for a moment. "Well, Kyle wasn't happy with him and Kyle is supposed to be one of his best friends. They were partners in Scott's business a long time ago and that partnership apparently dissolved at some point. But the reason I thought Kyle was upset with Scott was because Scott was flirting with Felicity. It seemed really obvious to me that Kyle held a torch for Felicity. Maybe even since they were in school together."

Burton jotted down more notes and then smiled at me. "You've been very observant during this crazy house party. Didn't you drink at all?"

I chuckled. "Sure, I did. Just not as much as everybody else did."

"Well, judging from all the hungover looking faces in there, they more than made up for the amount you didn't drink. Anybody else? Who am I missing? It sounds like the guy riled everybody in the house up."

I said, "Well, there's Roz and Grace."

Burton nodded. "You said Roz was a relative of Luna's?"

"Her cousin. And she was upset with both Kelly *and* Scott, but mostly Scott. It seemed like she was sick of the whole relationship between the two of them. She was frustrated that Kelly was dating this guy who seemed very toxic for her. They apparently had this on again, off again relationship and Roz was ready for it to be off again for good. She was fussing at Scott for his bad behavior most of the time—just looking out for Kelly."

Burton said, "And Grace?"

I considered this. "That's something I don't know much about. But there's something there. I was waking up from a nap on the boat at the time."

Burton's eyebrows flew up again. "Boat?"

"It was more of a yacht. But Grace rented it."

Burton gave a low whistle. "She doesn't seem to have a cash flow problem. But go ahead, I'm sorry. You were saying you were waking up from a nap on the boat."

"That's right. I had these mirrored sunglasses on so I opened my eyes but no one would be able to see I was awake. Scott and Grace were arguing. Well, it was more that Grace was arguing with Scott and Scott was acting self-satisfied."

"Could you make out what they were saying?"

"From what I could gather, Scott was saying that he knew some sort of information about Grace. He seemed to be threatening to disclose it at the party if she didn't do something."

Burton nodded. "Maybe he wanted her to pay him money. And why wouldn't he? He could easily see how well-off she was. Maybe that tempted him to try to blackmail her over whatever he knew about her."

I shrugged. "Who knows what he knew? Maybe it was even something from way back when they were teenagers or something. But Grace has her image now to think of. She wouldn't want to have that blown right when she moves back to her hometown."

"How did Grace respond to his threats?"

I said, "She was really cold to him. But she said she'd 'get it' for him, whatever it was."

Burton nodded again. "She was planning on going through with it, then. Or maybe she thought it would be easier just to get rid of him. Blackmail is hard to get out from under."

"The thing is that everything I've heard about Scott makes it sound like he was a pretty successful guy. I mean, he had his own business and everything. I can't really understand what would make him want to blackmail Grace."

"Maybe his business has taken a hit lately," said Burton. "That's something we'll be looking into, for sure."

We heard a lot of noise from the direction of the front door. Then we could hear the sound of sobbing.

Burton sighed. "That must be the girlfriend. We had an officer run over there to give her the news. We were going to go to her for an interview, but I guess she decided she wanted to come here, instead."

"They parted on such bad terms that maybe it makes her feel better to be here," I said. "Are you going to speak with her now?"

Burton shook his head. "Not while she's in that state. I'll speak to her after she's calmed down a little."

He stood up and I did, too.

"Thanks for all your help, Ann. This really helps me to ask better questions."

I winced a little. "I guess everyone will figure out that I was the one who helped you direct the questions better."

He chuckled. "You just gave me better perspective, that's all."

I hesitated. "I have a feeling I'm going to be grilled once I set foot out of the study. Is there anything I *shouldn't* say? Are you planning on revealing to everyone that it's murder?"

"Definitely. But I want to see everyone's reaction and that won't happen if everybody leaves the study and fills the others in. So how about if I announce it to the group now and you help me to see how everybody reacts?"

I followed him out the study door and he cleared his throat. Everyone abruptly stopped their conversations.

Burton said, "Thanks for your patience as I conduct these interviews. Since you're all here, I wanted to inform the group that we're treating Scott Haynsworth's death as a murder."

There were gasps around the room.

"But how?" stammered Grace. "We thought it looked as if he stumbled and hit his head on the way into the pool."

"It *could* have happened that way and I can understand your thinking that. But our team found a bloody champagne bottle that appears to be the murder weapon."

Chapter Seven

Everyone was stunned into silence this time. I saw Kelly looking blankly at Burton as if she couldn't understand what he'd said. Grace looked shattered, but she'd been looking shattered since we'd found Scott. Felicity's eyes were huge and she covered her mouth with her hand. Roz slipped an arm around Kelly to comfort her. And Kyle looked almost as blank as Kelly, as if he were trying to process what Burton just said. A tear slipped down Luna's cheek.

"Again, thanks for your patience. I'd like to speak with . . ." He glanced down at his notebook. "Kyle Hubbard next."

Kyle solemnly rose. I noticed his legs were unsteady underneath him and that he took a slight step back before following Burton to the study.

Kelly gasped, "I need some air." She bolted for the front door with Roz in tow. Luna hurried after her and, after a moment's hesitation, I joined them.

For a few minutes, we sat on the stone steps outside Grace's front door while Kelly gulped in the crisp fall morning air. After a little while, Kelly started to calm down a little, although her eyes were swollen with tears.

"How could this be?" she asked, looking down at the stone steps. "How did it come to this?"

Roz said quietly, "We're all so sorry, Kelly. I know what Scott meant to you."

"I've known him since we were kids! I mean, I know we had our problems, but we have always been there for each other. Who could have done something like this?"

Roz and I glanced at each other, probably thinking the same thing: that there were plenty of people who likely could have done it.

Luna, of course, had less of a filter. "He didn't deserve this, Kelly, but still . . . you know Scott was really acting out this weekend."

Kelly shot her a look but then slowly nodded. "Ann, you're probably totally baffled as to why I would go out with somebody who was acting like that. But you don't know how wonderful he usually was. When I say that we had our problems, they weren't *anything* like the way they were last night."

Roz glanced at me again. She apparently disagreed but didn't want to say anything in front of Kelly.

Kelly rubbed her eyes. "I'm just trying to figure out who did this. I mean, from what I'm guessing, it had to be somebody at the party, right?"

"That's what I understand," I said. It wasn't very likely that some stranger from Whitby would break in, bypass all the art and valuables, head right out to the pool room and assault Scott with a champagne bottle.

Another officer came out of the house. "I've just told the others, but I want to tell you as well. Once you've given a statement, you can go ahead and pack up your belongings and leave. Anything that you've left in the pool area must be picked up at a later date as we're still working the scene in there."

I glanced at Luna. I'd have to wait since Luna was my ride home and Burton hadn't spoken with her yet.

An hour later, we finally headed out. I'd hastily packed my bag as soon as Luna had given her statement.

Luna blew out a sigh. "That was the craziest house party ever. Are you ruined for life now? Will you ever leave your house or the library again?"

I chuckled. "No, the experience hasn't ruined me for life, although it wasn't exactly the restful, pleasant weekend we thought it was going to be."

"Well, that's good. I thought you were going to plan to lock yourself up in the library and throw away the key."

"No, I won't be doing that. Although I think I'm going to hang out at home the rest of the day with Fitz. My next-door-neighbor was looking in on him while I was gone."

And that was exactly how I spent the rest of the day. I pulled some weeds in the yard for a while. Fitz would swat at insects and watch as I yanked the weeds and put them in a pile. Then we went inside and Fitz curled up with me while I read my book.

There was a tap at my door about halfway through the afternoon and I carefully detached myself from Fitz and answered it. My heart beat just a little faster when I saw it was Grayson from down the street. I resisted the urge to fix the hair I knew was sticking up around my head and managed to give him a casual smile. "Oh, hi," I said.

He glanced inside and gave an apologetic chuckle. "Sorry, Fitz. Looks like you two were having some quiet time."

"Oh no, it's fine. We were just being lazy. What's up?" I winced inwardly. That made it sound like I was trying to hurry him off so I could get back to my book. "I mean, do you want to come inside?"

He shook his head. "Actually, I was just thinking that I wanted to go for a hike and was hoping to have you come with me. I'm trying to work some more exercise into my schedule, but I get really bored with the treadmill. Anyway, it's easier for me to follow-through if I have a walking buddy to go with me."

That's me. The buddy. I repressed the sigh that was threatening to blow out and gave him a bright smile. "Sure, that sounds great. Can you give me a couple of minutes to change clothes?"

"Sure. Maybe you could also recommend a good trail. I haven't been here long enough to really explore." He hesitated. "Are you sure you want to come along? I know this wasn't what you planned for your afternoon."

"No, it's perfect. I need some more exercise too and I've had kind of a stressful weekend. I'll tell you about it in a few minutes."

"I'll wait in the car," he said with a smile.

I rushed to the bedroom and managed to brush my wayward hair into some semblance of order in a ponytail. I put on my better-quality exercise clothes and put on the lightest amount of makeup . . . not wanting to look like I thought this was a date because it clearly wasn't. Then I gave Fitz a quick rub, refilled my water bottle, and hurried out to Grayson's car.

We talked casually for a few minutes as Grayson set out onto the mountain roads. I asked him what kind of hike he was looking for and mentioned a few options. One of them had a scenic waterfall along the way and he selected that one, which pleased me because it was one of my favorites.

He pulled off to the side of the road near the trailhead and we hopped out and started up the trail. He asked a few questions along the way about the shrubs and trees along the trail since he wasn't familiar with them from where he used to live. Then he said, "Hey, I forgot to ask you why you were stressed out."

"Sorry?"

"You know—when I mentioned going for a hike, you said that you'd had a stressful weekend so far," said Grayson, looking curiously at me. "Were you working this weekend and that's what made you stressed?"

I gave a short laugh. "Ironically, no—I was at a house party and trying to relax and *that's* what stressed me out."

Grayson slowed his pace and frowned. "Wait. You weren't at that lake party, were you? The one where someone died?"

I'd somehow forgotten that of *course* Grayson would know about the house party. He was an editor at the local paper. He'd have covered it. It would probably run in tomorrow's edition.

Grayson looked concerned and said in a gentler voice, "Hey, sorry for all the questions. I'm reporting on it, but I had no idea you were there. We're off the record, no matter what you tell me, I promise. If that's where you were, no wonder you got stressed. That must have been awful."

"It definitely wasn't what we were all expecting, that's for sure. And I feel bad for our hostess. She'd put a lot of time and energy into making it a relaxing weekend and it just . . . wasn't. And then someone died." I stopped and shrugged wordlessly.

"My understanding is the person responsible was someone at the party, too," said Grayson, slowly starting to walk again. "That must have been even worse . . . that it wasn't like some random stranger coming in." He looked quickly at me again. "We're off the record, of course."

"It put something of a damper on the party," I said dryly. "Realizing one of us was a murderer."

"Did it seem premeditated?" asked Grayson. He hurriedly added, "Look, if you don't want to talk about this, I totally get it. You came out on the hike to forget about everything for a while."

I'd have thought that I *wouldn't* want to talk about it, or at least not today. But surprisingly, I found I was eager to discuss it with Grayson. Maybe talking about Scott's death a little more with someone who wasn't at the party at all would help get it all out of my head for the rest of the day.

I hesitated and Grayson said, "Like I said, everything you tell me will be totally off the record. Although, if you tell me who the guests were at the party, I might approach them individually and see if I can get more information from them." He added hastily, "I wouldn't tell them how I knew they were guests there. And I'll only do it if you tell me it's okay."

I snorted. "We live in Whitby. For one thing, the guests will be telling everybody about the crazy party they went to the second they get back home. Then it's only a matter of time before the entire town knows."

I took a deep breath. "So, to answer your question, it didn't seem premeditated to me, but that's all I can tell you. I thought it was something that happened in the heat of the moment."

Grayson said, "Burton was able to give me the name of the victim since he'd already notified the family."

He didn't say anything else about the party and I felt myself relax again when we got to the waterfalls. It was a beautiful area, surrounded by trees and rhododendron. The sound of the water falling over the mossy rocks was almost deafening and we stood there silently for a minute, taking it all in. Grayson took out his phone again and took pictures, including one of me after waving off my protests and laughing at my unsuccessful attempts to smooth down my hair.

Then Grayson turned serious and my heart skipped a beat or two. "Do you mind if I ask you a question?"

Now my heart sped up and made up for the missing beats. "Of course you can." I wondered, could this have been a set-up for him to ask me out? To spend some casual time together and feel out how I might view that?

"Thanks," he said, looking at me warmly. "I've been thinking about this for a while, honestly. But I wasn't sure what you'd think. I know how busy you are at the library."

Was I giving off the impression that the library didn't leave me time to date? No wonder I wasn't getting any dates. I hastily said, "Not *that* busy. As a matter of fact, Luna and I were just talking about how it would be good for me to spend more time *out* of the library. I love it there, of course, but it tends to consume a lot of my life." I stopped short, realizing I was rambling and pressed my lips together before more words could slip out.

He grinned. "I know what you mean. It's like my job—I love the newspaper. I mean, I even love the smell of the place . . . the old papers and photographs. It makes me happy. But I can't hang out there *all* the time because then I wouldn't be able to follow up on leads or have information for articles. Anyway, what I wanted to ask was this: would you be interested in writing a column for the paper? On a regular basis, I mean?"

Chapter Eight

I felt my face fall and then quickly regained control.

Apparently not quickly enough, however, because his expression clearly reflected his concern. "Sorry . . . you don't want to, do you? Don't worry about telling me no. Believe me, I know how much you have going on at the library and the fact you're already writing a column for them: 'Ask Fitz', right? Plus you're running programs there and doing research and running away from our homeowner association president."

I gave him a weak smile. Avoiding Zelda Smith often in pursuit of Grayson and me. She was always trying to recruit new blood to the HOA leadership.

"I'd love to do it," I said, managing a better smile this time. And I was surprised that I meant it. Who knew—maybe it would give me more excuses for conversations with Grayson? Maybe this could be a common interest of ours. Maybe . . . it could lead to something else.

He beamed at me. "Really? That's great. I noticed the paper needed better regular content and I think this will work out perfectly for what I was thinking."

I asked, "What kind of content were you thinking about?"

He said, "That's why I was hoping you'd be able to fit this in. Because all I want you to cover is what's easiest for you to write. So that could be book recommendations for different genres, maybe a paragraph about upcoming events at the library, library services people might not know about, that kind of thing. I was hoping it wouldn't take too much time for you to write up."

It was honestly the kind of thing I could probably write in my sleep. All I did most of the day was to help patrons find good books, talk up events, and push library services.

"And if you had a time when you really couldn't think of anything, you could always just post a picture of Fitz," said Grayson with a grin.

I snorted. "That's exactly what we do on the library's social media accounts when we're at a loss. The sad thing is that a picture of Fitz lying on his back gets more engagement online than the posts we put a lot of time and thought into creating." I paused. "Since it sounds like I might be representing the library, I'm going to run this by my director, Wilson. But it's exactly the kind of thing he loves—more exposure for the library—so I'm pretty sure he'll want me to do it."

"That's great." There was a wooden bench a few yards away and Grayson settled on it and took his daypack off. He glanced up at me and smiled a little shyly. "I put a couple of sandwiches and some snacks in here just in case you said you'd come along on the hike. Would you like one? They're nothing fancy, just ham and cheese."

He pulled out a little cooler bag from the daypack and I nodded, sitting down next to him. I got out my water bottle and we sat there for a few minutes, eating and watching the water.

Watching a waterfall for me was almost like sitting on the beach and watching the ocean waves—super lulling and relaxing and somehow ever-changing. I could have sat there all day . . . especially with Grayson, even with our just-friends status.

After a while, Grayson brightened. "Hey, I just got another idea for a column."

I must have winced because he chuckled. "Don't worry, I won't pull you into this one." He tilted his head to one side thoughtfully. "Or will I?"

"What's this mysterious column?" I asked.

"I was just thinking that maybe other folks don't know a lot about the trails out here. Maybe they just moved here like me . . . maybe they just retired to the lake. Or maybe people in Whitby always choose the same hike because they know it well but they'd like the opportunity to try something different if they knew how strenuous or easy a trail was or what the views might be." Grayson talked quickly, warming to his subject.

I nodded. "That's probably true. I've been on most of them, I think, but that's because I grew up here. Still, I tend to choose the same trails over and over again. Like today—I thought immediately about the waterfall trail."

"So it might be fun if I choose a different trail every week and then talk about what it was like—how well the trail was marked, how difficult the walk was, how well it was maintained, how many people were hiking it that day, if there were spots for a picnic, what views were there along the way—stuff like that." He smiled at me and my heart melted just a little again. "That's where I thought you might want to come in. Maybe you could be my trail guide for at least some of them, since you're more familiar with them."

I considered this. In some ways, it sounded like I might be signing myself up for self-torture. Spending time with Grayson, but as friends. Or, really, hiking buddies.

He must have been able to read my conflicting feelings on my face because he hurriedly added, "Or maybe you could just even sit down with me and provide me with some ideas on where to start."

"I'd be glad to do that," I said. "When I was a teenager, my friends and I hiked just about every trail within thirty miles. I could give you a rundown of them." I hesitated. I didn't want to commit to going on the trails with Grayson, although I did want to spend more time with him and get to know him better. But I also didn't want to get hurt. "And if my schedule will let me, I'd be happy to go on a few with you, too."

He brightened. "That would be great, Ann. Thanks."

I was grateful that the rest of our hike together was easy. Not only because we were headed back downhill, but because we had a really easy-going conversation between the two of us.

After returning home from the hike, I really *did* take it easy. Fitz and I camped out on the sofa and I read more of *And Then There Were None* before finally turning on the television and zoning out in front of something silly, mindless and fun. I ended up turning in a couple of hours earlier than I usually do with Fitz curled up with me on the bed. As soon as I turned the light off, I must have fallen right to sleep because the next thing I realized, my alarm was blaring and the morning light was peeking through the blinds.

An hour later, I helped Fitz into the cat carrier and we set off for the library. I felt myself relaxing even more as I got out of the car and walked toward the building. It was a beautiful old Carnegie library in the Greek revival style and one of my favorite places anywhere. I had wonderful memories from when I was a kid with my great-aunt here at the library. I could remember getting my first library card and feeling so important and grown-up. I spent hours curled up reading Nancy Drew books in the children's section while my aunt copied recipes from the periodicals. It felt like home just as much as my house did.

As I walked up to the library, I slowed down. Someone had hung a poster of Fitz on the inside of the door. It was, of course, an adorable picture of Fitz looking especially welcoming. The poster had "Whitby Library" on it and "Fitz the Library Cat." It had to be Wilson's doing. He'd originally been a little doubtful about having a cat in the library, but had not only warmed to the idea but had practically made Fitz a member of the staff.

Wilson had beaten me in and hurried up to me as I walked in the door. I set Fitz's carrier on the floor and let him out.

"Thank goodness you brought the cat back. All the patrons were asking where he was all weekend. It was exhausting," said Wilson. "Maybe the next time you should just leave him at the library, instead. We could all chip in to feed him and empty his litter and whatnot."

I grinned at him. "That's what I was afraid of. I had the feeling I'd come back and Fitz would have gained five pounds from everyone feeding him." I tilted my head to one side. "I saw the poster of Fitz by the door."

Wilson looked proud. "Doesn't it look good? I thought it evoked a very warm welcome for the library."

"It certainly evokes a very cute one," I said with a snort.

Fitz, clearly knowing what side his bread was buttered on, flopped down in front of Wilson and rolled over on his back, purring. Wilson gave him a perfunctory scratch under his chin, but then capitulated when Fitz rolled back over and bumped Wilson's hand with his head.

I chuckled. "He wants you to pick him up."

Wilson looked uncertain about this.

"I brushed him last night and he won't shed. Your suit is very safe."

Wilson cautiously picked Fitz up and Fitz immediately curled his head under Wilson's chin. Wilson's face softened as he allowed himself a snuggle with the orange and white cat.

"Actually," said Wilson a bit gruffly, "I'm not only glad Fitz is back. It's very good to have you and Luna back, too." He glanced at the clock. "At least, I *suppose* Luna is coming back?"

Wilson was very punctual. He and I were both very much alike that way. I always felt if I wasn't fifteen minutes early, I was running late. Luna had a slightly more laid-back take on time which had caused Wilson some angst in the past. At this point, however, Luna was always right on time. Just not as early as Wilson and I always were.

"She'll be here," I said.

Wilson nodded, rubbing Fitz absently as he held him in his arms. "I had something of a brainstorm while you were both away."

"Did you?" I asked. I really hoped his brainstorm was that we needed more library staff. We'd been at a breaking point for a while. The library was a popular place, which I was delighted over, but we were so low on staff that it always felt we were scrambling. It was the sort of staffing situation where we were all in a real bind if someone was sick or wanted to take a day off. I'd mentioned this to Wilson for ages, but he always insisted we were in good shape. That our volunteers could help us bridge any staffing issues we had.

Wilson said, "That's right. I noticed our volunteers seemed to be running a little ragged while you two were gone. And there was frequently a line at the circulation desk, even with self-checkout. I think we're going to need to hire more staff."

I hid a smile. I loved the way Wilson acted as if he'd had a sudden realization, a moment of brilliance. That it was all his own idea. But however he presented it, I was vastly relieved to hear it. "I think you're right."

He nodded briskly, making Fitz move his head away from Wilson's chin and give him a reproachful look. "I certainly don't want to overtax our volunteers and it appeared they felt overwhelmed this weekend."

"If we don't have our volunteers to help shelve and check out patrons, we really will be in trouble. We definitely don't want to run them off." I paused. "What do you think about us hosting a volunteer appreciation day? Do you think we have funds in the budget for a small lunch? Something casual, maybe?"

Wilson brightened. "That's a marvelous idea. I could speak with our Friends of the Library and see if that's something their funds could cover. Otherwise, I'm sure there's likely a bit of excess money in our budget to handle it. I'll leave you in charge of the details, Ann."

I nodded, trying not to sigh. Naturally. This was usually where my bright ideas landed me . . . with more work.

Wilson's face suddenly flushed and he carefully put Fitz back down, brushing off non-existent cat fur from his suit jacket. I turned to see Luna coming in the library with her mother, Mona, in tow. Mona was carrying a tote bag.

The library phone rang and Wilson seemed to view it as being saved by the bell. "I'd better answer that." He hurried off in the direction of his office.

Luna rolled her eyes at me and Mona gave a frustrated sigh. "That man," she murmured.

"But you've made plenty of progress, Mom," said Luna.

"That's true." She brightened. "And I'm determined not to be pushy. I'm trying to be very subtle. You do think he likes me, though?"

"How could he help himself?" I asked with a smile. Mona was definitely an attractive woman. Smart, too. And she *wasn't* pushy. Wilson was just rather introverted and unsure about how to handle the situation. But I could tell he was warming to it all.

Mona reached into her tote bag and pulled out a plate carefully covered with plastic wrap. "A little bird told me Wilson was particularly fond of Rice Krispy treats, so I've made some."

"Do you want me to put them in his office?" I asked.

Mona shook her head vigorously. "Oh, no. Subtle, remember. But if you could put them in your breakroom, that would be wonderful. I've put a little note on there to indicate they're for everyone."

Luna said, "Maybe that will sweeten him up. Which he could definitely use."

Mona said, "I'm going to head off to the periodical section and work on my needlepoint for a while. Ann, if I lose track of time this afternoon, would you let me know when film club is about to start?"

I nodded. It still amazed me how Mona had become such great member of film club, which was a motley assortment of mainly male members of varying ages and interests. She always brought a unique perspective to the group and really helped facilitate discussion.

Plus, she sometimes brought snacks.

Mona patted her tote bag and said, "I made extra treats for the film club, since I already had all the ingredients out."

I chuckled. "You've already won them over, you know. Now they're going to be addicted to special treats. I always just make popcorn. Now they'll be spoiled and want something more elaborate."

"Which would be fine with me! I just need something to *do*. If it's baking, that's fine, too. I've just gotten tired of hanging around the house and not seeing people."

Luna gave her a hug. "You have no idea how happy I am to hear you say that." Mona, for a long time after a series of health problems, hadn't wanted to leave her house at all. But after Luna, who'd wanted to keep a closer eye on her mom, had started bringing her to the library during the day, she'd slowly come out of her shell.

Mona walked in the direction of the periodicals section, which was near a large gas fireplace. Fitz started bounding after her.

"Looks like you have company, Mona," I said.

She looked behind her and smiled. "Is it all right if I turn on the fire? It's a little nippy this morning and Fitz really enjoys it."

"Go ahead," I said. Soon there were going to be plenty of patrons here and they'd all want the fire on since it's such a chilly morning.

"I'd better go see what kind of shape the children's section is in," said Luna, wincing. "I have the feeling it might be a disaster since I've been gone a couple of days."

I said, "From what Wilson said, it was a madhouse here all weekend. Lots of patrons and the staff and volunteers couldn't keep up."

"So *definitely* a disaster." Luna blew out a sigh.

"For sure. But the good news is that Wilson said he's going to hire some more staff."

Luna lit up. "You mean he finally saw the light?"

"Apparently so. I guess it took both of us being gone on a busy weekend for him to make the connection that yes, we really *do* need an extra set of hands."

"So a full-time position."

I said, "I'm guessing so. That's what it sounded like." I glanced up. "He's heading back over here."

"Which is my cue to scurry out to clean up the picture books."

Luna started hurrying away, but Wilson raised a hand to stop her.

"I wanted to have a quick word with you both," he said.

Chapter Nine

"Uh-oh," breathed Luna. "Now what did we do?"

I frowned. "Is he . . . smiling?"

Wilson was. In fact, he was positively beaming. Never having seen quite such a delighted expression on his face, I wondered if he'd had a small stroke.

"The phone call I just took was someone interested in making a donation," he said.

Luna groaned. "Don't tell me. A complete collection of *National Geographic* magazines again."

"Or, perhaps, several hundred *Reader's Digest* condensed books?" I suggested.

Wilson shook his head, eyes glowing. "You're both wrong, for once. No, she wants to donate *money*."

"Money?" chorused Luna and I.

Wilson said, "Money. A real gift, too. Substantial." He frowned. "I'll have to figure out where those old gift record forms are. And the receipts for donor tax-deductions."

"Somewhere dusty, no doubt," I said dryly.

Luna asked, "What did she want the money to be used for?"

Wilson waved his hand in the air. "That's the best part of all. It's to be used at the *library's discretion*."

I blinked at him. "So not just for material acquisition?"

"It could be used for library services, program support, staffing, whatever we choose!" Wilson could barely contain his delight. I could see the wheels turning in his mind.

"Is this some sort of memorial? Or to honor someone?" I asked.

"Not a bit. But I understand I have both of *you* to thank," said Wilson, grinning at us.

Luna and I stared at each other.

"We have no idea what you're talking about," said Luna.

Wilson chuckled. "I must say you've been very cagey about it all. You must have had some sort of idea it was in the works. She surely said something to you about it."

"Who?" I asked.

"Grace Armstrong. I understand she was your hostess this weekend." He laughed again, which must have been a personal record. For Wilson, he seemed positively giddy. "If I'd only known, I'd have been a lot more thrilled about your weekend off."

Luna and I stared at each other again.

Wilson continued, "She said what great representatives of the library you both were. And that she'd been considering making some sort of donation to benefit the community for a while and decided on the library after speaking with you."

Luna said, still sounding doubtful, "Well, I guess she's moving back to Whitby after being gone for a long time. Making a donation that the community can all enjoy makes sense."

Wilson said, "I'm trying to think of how we should recognize her contribution. Perhaps we can name our community room the Grace Armstrong Community Room?"

I nodded. "That would certainly be easy enough."

Wilson added, "And maybe we could thank her in one of our online newsletters. And have a link in case anyone else feels they would like to make a contribution, themselves."

I could feel Wilson just getting cranked up on the whole program. It was likely going to turn into an entire movement.

"I don't know why we haven't focused on donations before," muttered Wilson, almost to himself. "Perhaps some people would like to even list the library in their wills. The library could be a beneficiary."

I glanced at Luna. We were losing him, I could tell.

"Just think of what we could do with more money!" Wilson's eyes lit up with glee. "More laptops for the computer area. We could update our technology. Purchase more periodical subscriptions. Buy educational toys for the children's department. Get software: language learning software or genealogy reference software. Update our furniture!"

He was on a roll. He started walking away from Luna and me, still muttering under his breath and likely on his way to make a list of all the ways the library could benefit from donations. Then he stopped short and whirled around. "And you two are having lunch with Grace today."

I blinked at him. "We are?"

"Indeed, you are. She asked if she could take you both to lunch and of course I said yes. *Any* time. She'll be here around noon." He strode off toward his office.

Luna and I stared at each other.

"What on earth was that about?" Luna rubbed her forehead.

"I don't really know. I didn't get the impression that either of us were great ambassadors for the library over the weekend, did you? I mean, people asked about what we did and we talked about it. I do love it here, so maybe some of my passion rubbed off. I gave Felicity and Grace a book recommendation. But it wasn't as if we were doing some sort of propaganda campaign to get guests to donate to the library."

Luna shrugged. "I guess it's like I was saying: she's back in Whitby and wants to do something to make her feel as if she's helping out the town in some way."

"It sure must have been a generous donation to have Wilson act like that. I've never seen him that way."

Luna nodded. "Yeah, he's on cloud nine." She tilted her head thoughtfully. "Maybe this is the right time for my mom to ask him out to dinner. I'm going to tell her."

She hurried off in the direction of the periodicals and I slowly got behind the circulation desk. I'd somehow thought that the oddness of the weekend was going to completely dissipate once I'd gotten into the safety of the library, but that wasn't proving to be the case.

Fortunately, the morning proved to be as busy as the weekend apparently had been. I helped several patrons with computer and cell phone questions, showed another patron an Excel spreadsheet tutorial, helped two women find something to read, and helped another find local resources to help with a job hunt.

Wilson came up to me shortly before noon. "Don't you need to be getting ready for lunch?" He frowned reproachfully at me.

"It's pretty busy up front," I replied. "And Grace isn't here yet."

"I'm sure she'll be here any minute. I'll take over the circulation desk, myself," he said briskly. "Go find Luna."

I wasn't sure how much preparation was required in getting ready for lunch, but when your manager asks you, you go.

Luna was shelving books and glanced up as I walked over. "We're to be getting ready for our lunch," I said dryly.

Luna knit her brows. "Getting ready? What on earth does that mean?"

I shrugged. "Maybe we're supposed to figure out what to say to Grace. I want to make sure she doesn't feel bad about the way her party went."

"No, she did everything right. She couldn't control what happened." Luna gave a little shudder.

"Do you think that's why she gave a donation to the library?" I asked. "It just seems sort of random. I'd gotten the impression she wasn't much of a reader."

"She's not," said Luna. "But maybe she wants to be. Or maybe she just liked what she heard about it. Or maybe she simply wants to make a contribution the whole community can enjoy."

"It must have been a sizeable one if Wilson is talking about new computers and furniture."

Luna said, "Yeah, but everything is relative, right? This is a woman who had a yacht with a captain for a weekend party.

Maybe the size of the donation didn't even seem big to her." She looked behind me. "Here she is now."

Luna and I both turned around with big, probably fake, grins as Grace walked toward us.

She gave us both a small hug and said, "Thanks so much for having lunch with me today. I hope your director didn't mind too much."

Luna snorted. "Mind? He's practically shoving us out the door. We hear you gave an incredibly generous gift to the library."

"Thanks so much for that," I added quickly, trying to be the library ambassador Wilson would want me to be. "Wilson is totally over the moon about it and figuring out which areas might benefit the most."

Grace waved her hand in a dismissive gesture. "It was nothing. I'm just glad you were both there this weekend to talk about what a great place the library is for the whole community. Somehow, I was still thinking it was mostly just about old, outdated books. But you're really helping out in a lot of ways."

Again, thinking about Wilson I said, "I could give you a really quick tour, if you have time? Sort of highlight some of the different things we do here?"

Luna gave me a thumbs-up in approval.

Grace said, "That would be great! It would help me visualize more of what goes on at the library. Then I'd like to treat you both to lunch."

Luna said, "Oh, Grace, you've done too much already. Ann and I can pay."

Which we definitely could. Depending on where Grace wanted to go, however, Luna and I might choose to just eat appetizers or a cheap salad, though.

Grace shook her head. "No way. My treat. After all, I want to apologize about the weekend."

Luna and I both started protesting at once.

"No, really. Anyway, we'll talk about that later. Now for the tour," said Grace.

So we showed Grace the community room and gave her a rundown of all the different programs for the different age groups we held there. We showed her the computer room and explained the demographics of the patrons who used it and how we held classes there to improve computer literacy. We showed her the different types of media that could be checked out and the online programs patrons could use. Wilson spotted us showing Grace around and looked enormously pleased.

Then we were off to lunch. As I'd halfway anticipated, Grace decided on the nicest place in town . . . which was decidedly *not* Quittin' Time, my usual spot to grab a quick, inexpensive meal.

We sat down and Grace immediately ordered us all appetizers for the table to share. Then we placed our meal order. She offered to buy us wine and Luna and I quickly turned it down.

"I'd nod off during film club," I said dryly.

Grace laughed and ordered herself a glass of white. She took a deep breath. "I just wanted to say I was sorry for the way the weekend turned out. I feel awful about it."

Chapter Ten

Luna reached out and gave Grace a quick hug. "We feel awful about it, too! Ann and I were just saying earlier that you put so much time and energy into the weekend and it wasn't fair to you that it turned out the way it did."

"I still had a great time," I added. And parts of it *had* been great.

Grace smiled at us. "I really appreciate your saying that."

"You couldn't control what your guests did, after all," said Luna stoutly. "Or guest, singular, anyway."

"You're right. But I never should have invited Scott in the first place. My mother-in-law used to always say that the guest list was the most important thing about party preparation. I should have realized that inviting him would be a recipe for disaster. But Kelly wanted him there and I thought he wouldn't be drinking as much as he was." She shrugged and gave a short laugh. "Clearly, I underestimated him and then tragedy happened. I feel terrible because the two of you work really hard and both deserved a break."

Luna seemed uneasy about accepting this accolade. "Well, I work *pretty* hard. Lots of hours, for sure. Ann works *ridiculously* hard."

Grace gave me an apologetic look. "Here you thought you were going to have a short getaway and it ended up being something completely different."

I shook my head firmly. "No more apologizing, Grace. I appreciate it, but it isn't needed, I promise."

Our appetizers came and for a few minutes Grace and I divvied up the meaty plates to share while Luna sampled the vegetarian ones. I didn't know when I'd seen such a spread of food. Then I realized: I'd seen it at Grace's. This must be how she ate all the time. I wondered how she stayed so slim. Shrimp with avocado and tomato, bruschetta, potato cakes, a vegetable plate, duck and dumplings, and steak tartare.

After a few minutes of exclaiming over our appetizers, Grace deflated again. "I guess the reason I'm so fixated on the weekend and feeling bad about it is because I feel responsible." She lifted a hand. "Don't worry—I know I wasn't really responsible for what happened. But maybe I could have stopped what happened to Scott."

I shook my head. "Grace, there was no way you could have done that."

"I might have. I was so worn out from all the conflict and tension that I slept like a rock. But if I'd been more on top of things, maybe paid attention to what was happening downstairs, perhaps I could have stopped whoever did this."

Luna swallowed down a large gulp of her food. "Grace, you need to stop thinking like that."

I added, "Who knows what might have happened if you tried to step in? You might have been killed or severely injured, yourself."

"Maybe I could have at least called the police," said Grace with a small shrug. "But instead, this happened while I was dead asleep in the bed."

Luna said, "Yeah, well, it happened when *we* were asleep, too, and Ann and I don't feel guilty about it. Neither should you."

Grace rubbed her head as if it hurt. "I appreciate that. The truth is, I'm reconsidering what my motive was in even having this party."

Their entrees arrived and Grace waited while the waitress set it all down and refilled their glasses. Ann, already full from the appetizers, was thinking she might be able to manage a few bites before putting the rest in a to-go box to sit in the library break-room fridge for supper at home.

Grace continued thoughtfully, "Part of it was a genuine desire to have folks enjoy themselves, catch up with their old friends, and meet some new people. I've always loved meeting different kinds of people. It's what makes life interesting, right? So I wanted to catch up with people I knew growing up, but I was glad to meet you, Ann, and get to know Luna better."

Luna added, "And you just finished your house. Of course you wanted a housewarming party."

Grace nodded. "That's part of it, too. The construction took a lot longer than I thought it would and was a lot harder. I had a really naïve idea about the whole process, you know?"

I smiled at her although I had absolutely no idea about either building or redecorating a home since I'd moved right into my great-aunt's house, felt it reflected who I was, and barely changed a thing.

"I thought it would be this amazing creative challenge of colors and textures. But really, it was a much more pedestrian process of following up with missing contractors and having to pick another type of rug when one was discontinued. The minutiae of finials and blind pulls." She shook her head as if to clear it.

I said, "I don't know much about any of that, but our library does have a ton of resources on decorating."

Grace laughed. "See? That's exactly why I should have had a closer relationship with the library from the start."

Luna said, "Well, you sure have a close relationship with it, now. Wilson is your best friend."

"I'll be sure to be over there more now that I know what I'm missing. Anyway, I'm sorry I'm going off on a tangent. The point is that part of me had really good motives for the weekend. But part of me maybe didn't." Grace shrugged unhappily. "I feel like part of me almost *wanted* to stir the pot a little bit. I mean, I knew that some of the personalities I'd invited over might not mesh well." She sighed. "I'm addicted to those reality shows where they put strangers in a house together and watch them blow up. Maybe part of me wanted to see the drama."

Luna wouldn't accept this. "Nope. I don't think you did that at all. You were a peacemaker the whole time. I saw it. You were trying to calm everyone down, distract us with great food. You did a good job, Grace."

Grace said, "Well, I tried, anyway. I felt bad for everyone. Scott was being really vile and maybe I should have just told him he was uninvited to my party. Especially when Kelly left. And I felt terrible for Felicity, too. She told me Scott was coming on too strong and she was trying to get away from him."

I was surprised at this. The flirting that I'd seen Scott do seemed mostly to taunt both Kelly and Kyle. I'd gotten the impression he was doing it for effect, to try to get under his friends' skin, and didn't have much interest in Felicity at all. At any rate, Felicity seemed totally able to deflect it. I must have missed something over the weekend.

The waitress returned to check on us and Grace used the opportunity to quickly change the subject. She asked more about the library programs and community turnout and how we used Fitz in social media to get attention for various events. Luna and I filled her in and conversation felt light and easy after that. Luna was somehow able to knock out her spinach and ricotta Rotolo, but the waitress took the rest of my primavera to box it up for me.

Luna got up to find a restroom before we headed back to the library. As soon as she was out of earshot, Grace leaned over to speak to me.

"What do you think about Roz?"

"I don't know her very well," I prevaricated. "I've mainly spoken with her when she's run by the library to see Luna. I've always liked her."

Grace nodded thoughtfully. "Yes. I always have, too. I was surprised to see how much she was drinking, though. I don't remember her being like that when we were in high school."

"Was she drinking too much over the weekend?" Again, I hadn't gotten that impression at all. Everybody was drinking more than they probably usually did, but the only person I'd noticed get sloppy drunk was Scott. Although Roz had definitely dispatched those two big glasses of champagne pretty quickly.

"I don't want to say it was *too much*, but it was a lot."

I said slowly, "But she turned in early, right. Directly after Kelly left."

Grace nodded. "And I did, too, of course. But Roz ended up getting back up again."

I stared at her. "I didn't realize that."

"Your room wasn't near the pool room. Mine, and Roz's actually, are right above where the pool skylight is. I could hear Roz having an argument with Scott."

"You think Roz is responsible for Scott's death?" I asked.

Grace shook her head quickly. "I can't say that. She might very well have gone down, told Scott off, and then headed straight back to her room. I went back to sleep after I saw it was her. All I know is that Roz has always been very protective of Kelly, even when we were back in school. Maybe she got angry with Scott and picked up the closest thing to hand. Maybe she was so intoxicated that she doesn't even remember it."

I still couldn't quite get past the fact that Grace believed Roz was a lot drunker than I remembered her being. "Roz didn't seem like she'd had that much to drink, though. Definitely not enough to cause a blackout."

Grace nodded. "I know. She was more careful when she was around us. I think Kelly doesn't like to see her get really intoxicated and tries to look out for her. But I know Roz packed her own beverages in her bag. I went by her room before we all had supper and although she tried to hide it, I saw a bottle in her overnight bag."

Any further discussion of this was abruptly stopped as Luna came back to the table, blissfully unaware of what we'd been discussing.

"That was the best meal ever," she said, patting her stomach in satisfaction. "Although I might not ever eat again; I'm stuffed. Let's hope I don't fall asleep when we get back to the library. I'll have to raid the coffeemaker in the breakroom."

Grace laughed. "I don't envy you. I'm going to head back home and take a quick nap. Or maybe a *long* one."

She paid the bill, waved away our thanks, and took us back to the library.

We were about to get out of the car when Grace said, "I didn't realize you had a library dog as well as a library cat."

I peered out the window. Sure enough, there was a large dog of indeterminate heritage and a sweet face looking plaintively at the car.

"Oh, the poor thing!" said Luna. "She looks like she's lost."

I made a face. "There's no way Wilson would let us to have a library *dog*. He was barely sold on Fitz at the time. Let's take some pictures of her and post them in the library. Maybe someone knows who she belongs to."

Grace laughed, "Good luck with all of that. And thanks for having lunch with me. I'll see you both soon."

She left and Luna and I snapped a few photos of the dog, who was incredibly friendly. She came up and nuzzled their hands until they petted her, then flopped down on her back for a tummy rub.

"No collar," I said. "Maybe if she's still here after work one of us can run her to the vet to check for microchips."

Luna said, "And I'll look online at the missing pet sites and see if she fits any descriptions on those."

I walked in to connect my phone with the computer and make a "found" poster. Wilson came right up to greet me as soon as I came in.

"How did lunch go?" he asked with an air of both anticipation and concern.

I grinned at him. "Don't worry, Luna and I didn't do anything to mess up the donation. We had a great lunch and a very friendly talk with Grace. I think you saw that we gave her a tour of the library. She was super enthusiastic about our programs and the facility."

Wilson gave a small sigh of relief. "That's good. Well, feel free to have lunch with her at any time. Or dinner. Or whatever she'd like."

He started walking away and I said quickly, "I did have something to ask you real quick. I saw Grayson from the newspaper yesterday. He asked if I could do a regular column for the paper. Since I'd be representing the library, I thought I'd better run it by you first."

Wilson, as I'd expected, perked up again. "I think that's a great idea. And be sure to mention Fitz. Maybe even run some pictures of him, too. We can always use the publicity."

"I'll call him then and tell him it's a go." I paused. "Speaking of Fitz, did you know there's a dog hanging around outside?"

Wilson frowned. "What does that have to do with Fitz?"

"Well, nothing, I suppose. Except that Fitz came to us as a stray and now there appears to be a stray dog who's also shown up at the library."

Wilson shook his head. "No more animals here. Can you figure out who it belongs to? Or find it a good home?"

I nodded. "I'm already on it. Luna and I have taken some pictures of her."

"Yes, post them everywhere. On our social media, too." Wilson made a face. "It wouldn't look good if we called animal control to collect the dog. We don't want to be in the position of being the bad guys, but we also don't need a dog here. Period."

He headed off to the office and I transferred the photos from my phone to the computer and came up with some flyers. The desk phone rang and I picked it up. "Whitby Library."

It was Grayson. I was annoyed at the red flush I felt creeping up my neck.

"Oh good, I got you, Ann. I realized I don't have your cell phone number so I figured I'd see if I could get you at work. Am I interrupting anything?"

"No, it's fine. No one's at the desk right now. Actually, I was just thinking about you." I flushed again and hurriedly added, "That is, I just spoke with Wilson, my director. He gave me the green light for the column."

"That's great news! Hey, I was wondering . . . I know this is last minute, but do you think you could have something in a couple of days? I've got a piece running on historic downtown buildings and the library is going to be included. I thought your column might be a nice piece to accompany it."

Grayson was clearly used to coming up with articles at the spur of the moment. I thought for a moment and said, "Sure, that shouldn't be a problem. But what kind of article are you looking for?"

"Anything you want," said Grayson expansively. He must have meant this to be encouraging, but the number of possible directions I could go in made the assignment seem totally overwhelming.

I said, "How about this: I'll write something that's sort of an essay at the top, then mention upcoming library programs and give a book recommendation at the bottom. Would that format be okay? That way it's a little bit of everything."

"Sounds perfect. Any ideas for the essay part?"

One thing came to mind quickly. I frequently had to read books that I didn't pick myself—that were recommendations from patrons who wanted to share their favorite books with me. "Maybe something on books we feel obligated to read, don't really enjoy at the beginning, and then like later on. You know—books that family gifts us, books that friends gush over. I was tasked with reading *Ulysses* not long ago and hated the thing until I was about halfway through."

Grayson chuckled on the other end. "So you're one of those people who advocates for sticking with a book, even if you don't really get into it right away."

"Actually, no, I'm not. Totally the opposite, in fact. There are far too many books out there for us to read in our lifetimes, even if we read all day long. If you don't connect with a story, try something else. Better yet, always get your books from the library so you haven't even made a financial investment in the story and won't feel bad about abandoning it."

"I like that you worked a plug for the library in the middle of that." Grayson's voice was teasing and I flushed again.

"Apparently, I can't help myself," I said dryly. "Anyway, will that work?"

"It sounds great. But you don't have to pass all your ideas by me—that's why I picked you for the column. I know you'll do a good job."

I saw Linus, one of my favorite patrons, walking in the direction of the desk and said, "I'd better run. I'll send it over to you as soon as I'm done."

Linus was retired, but always neatly dressed in an immaculate suit. He'd lost his wife just a few years before. He wore large spectacles that lent him an owlish expression. He loved a routine and had been coming here daily since his wife had passed, reading the library's newspapers in the morning, segueing to fiction, then nonfiction. He always left at precisely noon for lunch, returning forty-five minutes later. He'd always been perfectly polite, but had never spoken beyond *good morning* until Luna drew him out when she started working here. Now, he and I had become friendly in a quiet way.

"Hi, Linus," I said with a smile.

He smiled back. "Hi." He cleared his throat. "I was wondering about the dog outside."

Chapter Eleven

"The dog." I winced. "I hope she didn't bother you. Jump on you or something?" I glanced at his suit and thought that muddy paws would certainly do a number on it.

He shook his head. "Not at all. But I was just wondering about her."

"She showed up while I was away at lunch. No collar or tags. I think I'm going to have to get her to the vet to see if she has microchips. And I've made up some flyers."

Linus nodded thoughtfully. "But won't the veterinarian's office be closed by the time you get out of the library?"

"Good point." Obviously I hadn't had my thinking cap on. There *are* places in town that are open normal business hours, but the library isn't one of them.

Luna hurried up to us, looking warily over her shoulder toward Wilson's office door. "Is the coast clear?"

Linus and I stared at her. "Clear for what?" I asked.

She held up a tote bag she was holding and pulled out a plastic container. "To feed the dog out there."

I frowned. "Is that your lunch?"

"It's the lunch I packed for myself today before I realized I was going out for a tremendous, fancy meal. Don't you think he'll be okay eating sweet potatoes, broccoli, and carrots?"

I looked the foods up on my computer. "Looks like they'll be fine to give dogs. Maybe go light on the broccoli, since that's a lot of fiber."

"Okay. Better run while Wilson's not around." Luna turned toward the door.

Linus said hesitantly, "I could help. If you need help."

"Sure!" Luna beamed at him.

Linus said, "And I can take her to the vet to check for microchips, too." He flushed. "Since I believe you're both getting out after the vet may have closed?"

"Sure thing! That would be great, Linus. Okay, let's do our secret food mission real quick. We'll find out if this dog likes vegetables or not."

While they were outside, I helped a student find a couple of books he needed for a report he was working on. When I walked back over to the circulation desk, Luna was back.

"What happened to Linus?" I asked.

"You won't believe this, but he's gone to the store to get a harness and a leash." She held up her watch so I could see it. "And it's almost two o'clock! It's time for him to be sitting over in the periodical section reading nonfiction or something. You know what a tight schedule he puts himself on."

I said slowly, "That's pretty amazing. Honestly, not following his routine is almost alarming. If he didn't show up at the library one day, I wouldn't hesitate to call Burton to do a wellness check on him."

"Same." She looked at the door and shook her head.

"Maybe he's tired of being alone," I offered. "He has a pretty solitary day for a guy who spends his day in a very public place."

Luna nodded. "He only comes over to talk every now and then. And it's never for very long."

"Maybe he and the dog hit it off?" I asked.

Luna thought about this for a moment. "He did talk to her in a very low voice for a while and she whimpered back to him. Yeah, they did sort of hit it off."

"I would think owning a dog would be one way to avoid being alone without having to totally change your usual routine by reaching out to other people, making friends, that sort of thing."

"Exactly," said Luna. "And now I'm hoping that nobody steps forward to claim the dog. I mean, she's a sweet animal and didn't complain at all about eating somebody's cold vegetables. I grabbed one of Fitz's extra water bowls and put it out there near the bushes, too. Hopefully all under Wilson's radar."

We both looked in the direction of his office. "He's been in there since we came back. I think he's dreaming up ways of spending the library windfall," I said.

I glanced at the clock. "Hey, I've got to go ahead and start setting up the community room for film club."

"Oh, right. Remember, that's the future Grace Armstrong Community Room, ha. You've got somebody else presenting today?"

"Timothy." I grinned at Luna. "It should be good."

"Well, I know Mom is looking forward to it. She thinks Timothy is amazing."

"He is, for sure." Timothy was a lovable, gangly home-schooled high school kid who was truly an old-soul. He didn't relate to his peer-group very well, but he was warmly embraced by the motley assortment of folks in the library film club. There he found people who seemed to get his interest in classic films and difficult books. He was the one who'd set me on the course to read *Ulysses*.

"What movie did he pick?" asked Luna. "I could kind of see him going with *Blade Runner* or something like that."

"He might have picked that, but I think he was trying to defer to the different folks in the group. He picked *The Princess Bride*."

Luna grinned. "Oh, my gosh, that's one of my all-time favorites. I wish I could sneak in there and watch it." She cast a glance over at the children's section. "But I've got to get back over there before it starts really getting busy. Have a lot of people in the group seen it?"

"Actually, it sounded like just a couple had, which is pretty amazing. I think it's one of those things where it's been on everybody's list to watch, but no one really had."

"Well, they're in for a treat," said Luna. She frowned. "Actually, I'm not sure my mom has even watched it. It's going to be right up her alley."

I started setting up for the club meeting, pulling out chairs and setting up the computer to show the movie. After a few minutes, Timothy came in to give me a hand.

He grinned at me. "I'm really pumped about this movie today. Hope we have good turnout from the club."

I said, "There may be some newcomers here, too. I had a really good response on social media when I did a post about the movie."

He laughed. "Yeah, I saw it. Fitz made it practically go viral."

Fitz was sitting with a toy sword in the post. He'd looked fetching, as usual.

I was glad to see Timothy seemed totally relaxed and excited about talking about the film instead of being worried about speaking in front of a group. Since he'd joined film club, I'd watched him really come out of his shell.

A few minutes later, members started filing in, joking with each other and catching up. Mona came in, too, and sat up front.

"I've heard so many good things about *The Princess Bride* that I want a front-row seat," she said with a smile.

I noticed that this time she hadn't brought any knitting to work on. That was a good sign.

Timothy said, "I still can't believe you haven't seen it. You're going to love it."

Aside from our regulars, I saw some new faces, probably due to the Fitz ad. I greeted them all and gave them a little print-out of upcoming films in case they wanted to join us again. I was surprised to see Kyle come in, but went quickly over to greet him.

"Thanks for coming by," I said to him.

He gave me a smile, but I noticed his eyes were tired. "You made it sound fun, so I thought I'd give it a go."

"We've got a little bit of a different setup this time," I said and explained how different members were sharing their favorite films. I introduced him to a few of the other members. Then I pointed out where the popcorn was and the lemonade and he settled into a chair as Timothy dimmed the lights and got us started.

The group was very receptive to the movie and were laughing uproariously at parts. I glanced over at Timothy and saw how pleased he was. After the film was over, he gave some background and some trivia about the movie and started off what ended up being a great discussion.

I saw Wilson peering in through the window at one point, seeming pleased by the response. I smiled as I saw his gaze pause on Mona before he quickly glanced away.

I walked over to Kyle, who was looking my way. "How did you like it?"

"Oh, I've seen it a lot of times. But the discussion was great and I loved the kid's rundown on the trivia and the making of the film. The background he gave was really solid."

"Thanks. I'll be sure to share that with him," I said.

Kyle shook his head. "You don't have to—I'll tell him myself." He grinned. "I'm just waiting for a chance."

Timothy was indeed surrounded by film club members telling him what a great job he'd done and talking more about the film. They appeared to be suggesting that they all come dressed up as one of the characters from the movie when Halloween rolled around.

After a while, the members filed out. Kyle spoke to Timothy and then Timothy left to catch up with someone who'd pulled out a book they thought he might like. It was just me and Kyle and I was putting the chairs away.

"I can give you a hand with these," he offered.

And I gladly let him, since it took half the time to get the chore done.

But I still thought it very coincidental that he'd chosen to come to film club and was lingering so long. It seemed to me that he had something on his mind.

"How have you been?" I asked.

He didn't ask what I meant by that. "Okay, I guess. I don't know. I've felt really bad about Scott's death. Like I should have been able to help him somehow. We'd been friends since we were kids. We went to college together and into business together after that. I've known him forever."

It seemed like guilt was the common factor feeling of everybody I'd talked to. "What could you have done, though? If you'd tried to stop a murder, you might have ended up getting hurt, yourself."

He shook his head. "I knew Scott was in a bad way and I should have escorted him up to his room or something. He definitely shouldn't have been *swimming*. He might have listened to me if I'd told him he should sleep it off."

I said in a reasonable tone, "But it wasn't the swimming that was the problem."

"No, it was really his attitude that was the problem. And somebody there'd had enough. See, that's something else I could have helped with. I could have even driven him back home. He wasn't usually that bad, you know. I guess I was as stunned as everybody else was. But when it happened, I wasn't helping him at all. I was *sleeping*." His voice was bitter.

"Of course you were. I was, too. It had been a big day with lots of food, sun, and alcohol."

"And stress," added Kyle with a wry smile.

"That too. Which made everybody even more exhausted. There's nothing more tiring than stress."

Kyle said, "I couldn't even fall asleep right away because I was so wound up. I had to have time to decompress by myself. I watched part of a movie on my phone in my room for a while so I could relax enough to fall asleep."

"Did you hear anything while you were still up?"

Kyle shook his head. "Nope. I was no help at all. The cops were asking me the same thing. 'Was there someone outside in the hall while you were up?' And I don't have any clue because I had my earbuds in. I was trying to keep quiet so everybody else could sleep. I was distracting myself with a movie so I wouldn't be tempted to go downstairs to the pool and beat Scott up." He made a face. "That's another reason I feel guilty. It's not just that I couldn't help save his life. It's also that, even though he's dead, I'm still pretty angry at him."

"That's probably natural. He wasn't being a great friend that day, after all."

"No. Not to me and not to anybody else there. Especially Kelly." Kyle rolled his eyes.

"I understood they usually weren't that bad together."

Kyle said, "Well, there are different levels of bad. They were usually *nothing* like they were over the weekend. I went out with them for lunch fairly often. But they've always had these really animated random arguments. I mean, those two could argue over anything. Even stuff that should really just be a friendly, academic argument. I heard them arguing over the best Disney movies, for crying out loud."

I chuckled and Kyle nodded. "Right? I mean, totally ridiculous. And it might start out as something *sort of* friendly, then it would escalate and the next thing you knew, it would get really heated. Those two were volatile, especially when they were together. I guess when things were good between them, things were good. But most of us saw the craziness. I worried they'd end up married. Who could live that way every day, together?"

He looked thoughtful for a moment and continued, "So everybody apparently is saying they were asleep. Everybody. But someone in the group wasn't sleeping at all. Someone got up, went downstairs, and hit Scott's head with a bottle."

I nodded. "Did you have any ideas?"

He sighed. "I don't know. After all, I grew up with these folks. I don't think of any of them as a killer. The only thing I can imagine is that somebody lost control. Scott pushed the wrong person's buttons one time too many, you know? Maybe they'd had too much to drink, too, and weren't thinking straight. They grabbed the closest thing to hand which would, of course, be a champagne bottle since there were gobs of them down there. Then they freaked out and ran off." He glanced over at me. "I can't help but wonder if maybe it was Kelly."

"Kelly? But Kelly wasn't there."

"Wasn't she?" Kyle snapped his lips together as if he were annoyed with himself for saying that much.

"What do you mean? Did Kelly come back later on?" I was starting to wonder how on earth I'd managed to sleep so soundly there.

He sighed and rubbed his face with his hands. "She came back before I headed upstairs for the night. She was furious. Scott had sent her a text message breaking up with her."

I made a face.

"Exactly. I mean, who does that? It's kind of an eighth-grade move. I'm actually really surprised Scott would do something like that." He frowned. "Actually, *he* seemed a little surprised. Maybe he was so drunk at the time that he sent it that it totally slipped his mind."

"Maybe so," I said. "But he didn't seem like the kind of guy who tried avoiding conflict by breaking up via text."

"Right. He had plenty of conflict over the weekend—why not have more?"

I said, "So Kelly came back. But she ended up leaving Grace's house and heading back home again. And yesterday morning, she seemed really stunned about Scott's death. And upset."

"I'm sure she *was* upset about it. She's known Scott all her life. Was she stunned?" Kyle shrugged. "She seemed to be."

"So, the question is, did Kelly end up back home again before or after Scott died?"

"No idea. Like I said, I went upstairs, watched a movie on my phone for a while to chill out, and then fell asleep. Who knows what happened the rest of the night?"

"Did you tell the police about this?" I asked slowly.

"Nope." My expression must have been very disapproving because he laughed. "Look, Ann, I didn't have any proof that Kelly did anything at all besides have an argument with Scott. She ended up back at her own place. It's up to her to come clean

. . . and maybe she did. Anyway, the cops would have Scott's phone, so they'd see he sent her that text message. Besides, Kelly is my friend. That doesn't mean I don't see her faults and she doesn't see mine. It doesn't mean I don't criticize her to her face about the kind of guys she chooses over and over again to go out with. But it does mean she can expect to have my back."

I was still processing this and realizing I was going to have to go to Burton with the information when Kyle gave me a be-seeching look. "I had a question to ask you."

"Sure."

"You were talking with Felicity about a nonfiction book club when we were at the party. She said she was going to try to make it there. Could you tell me with club it was? I looked on-line and there seemed to be a couple of them."

I tried to remember which one I'd recommended to Felicity. "I believe it was one that focused on short nonfiction reads for busy people."

"Sounds perfect," said Kyle wryly. "When does it meet?"

"Once a month on Mondays. I think the next meeting is next week," I said.

Kyle looked cheerful. "Thanks for that." He paused. "It's just that the way you described the club made it sound very appeal-ing."

Right. So appealing that he couldn't even remember which club it was. I just nodded and gave him a wave as he headed out the door, practically skipping away.

Chapter Twelve

I locked up the community room and headed over to the circulation desk since there was usually a little rush over there after film club wrapped up, with most of the members being good readers, too. Sure enough, five or six of them came over with books and conversation and we chatted for a while. I noticed Mona was hanging back with an eye to Wilson's office.

She came up to talk after the others had filed out.

"Did you enjoy the movie?" I asked.

"I loved it! It had a little bit of everything. Great story." She glanced over toward Wilson's office again and whispered, "Any sign of him today?"

I shook my head. "Honestly, he hasn't been out much. He's really excited about this gift the library got."

Mona nodded. "Luna was telling me about that. And about your lunch."

I grimaced. "I just realized—what did *you* do for lunch? You've been here all day."

She chuckled. "Oh, I brought my lunch, too. That's my usual routine. Luna packs her messy veggie stuff in her box and I make myself a sub sandwich to put in mine. I can't eat in the breakroom, of course, but usually she and I will take a short walk to the park and sit on one of the benches there and eat."

"I see. I'd never really thought about the logistics of how you two handled that—I guess because Luna and I are usually eating lunch at different times."

"Except today for the special lunch," said Mona, eyes twinkling. "I'm amazed, after all you probably ate, that you didn't doze off in front of the movie."

"Which is a real testament to how good *The Princess Bride* is," I said dryly. "Believe me, I probably ate enough for several days. And I still brought a take-out container for supper tonight."

"Well, I'm glad you two were able to do something nice today after the weekend you had. What a dreadful discovery. And Luna had been so excited that you were finally going to relax and have a fun weekend." Mona made a face.

"It was a shock, for sure. But the weekend wasn't all bad. I'm sure Luna gave you some of the highlights."

"The ship and the food. Oh, and the amazing house. Grace certainly did well for herself after leaving Whitby," said Mona.

"Her family wasn't wealthy?"

"Goodness, no. They lived a very modest life. Both of them are gone now, you know. Her mother passed away from cancer some years ago and her father from a heart attack," said Mona. She stopped abruptly upon hearing a sound from the direction of Wilson's office. "Is he finally emerging?"

I glanced over. "It appears so. Want me to find an excuse to flag him down?"

"Would you? I'm trying so hard not to be a pest that I'm hardly speaking to him at all."

So I lifted my hand to signal Wilson and he hurried over.

"I spoke with Grayson at the paper and have already got my first assignment. It's going to run in the next few days," I said to him.

"Excellent," beamed Wilson. "That should give us some nice coverage."

"Besides the column, I'm going to add in some of the upcoming programs. Have there been any changes to the ones that are currently posted online?"

A trumped-up excuse or not, it was good I'd asked because apparently there *had* been some program changes. Wilson knew them by heart and I jotted them down as he read them out.

Mona was looking nervous and I quickly said, "Wilson, have you made it to the breakroom at all today? I know you've been busy in your office figuring out how best to manage Grace's gift."

Mentioning the gift might have been a mistake. I could see by Wilson's expression that his thoughts were already drifting back to his spreadsheets and lists. He said absently, "No, as a matter of fact, I haven't. I'd packed a lunch and ate it in my office."

I said, "You're missing out, then. Mona brought by Rice Krispy treats this morning."

His eyes lit up and he turned to Mona. "Did you? Those are my favorites, actually. I'll definitely be stopping by the breakroom now."

Mona smiled shyly at him and said, "And have plenty. I'm sure Luna would have already broken into them by now, but she's so stuffed from her lunch that I'm wondering if she'll ever eat again."

Wilson looked distracted again by the mention of the lunch, but managed to rein his attention back to Mona. "That was very kind of you to bring them by." He hesitated. "Did you go to the film club meeting? You usually make those, don't you?"

She nodded. "*The Princess Bride.*"

Wilson said, "I've heard that's very good, but I've never seen it."

"Oh, you must! It's probably streaming somewhere. You should definitely watch it."

Wilson said wryly, "The problem is that I haven't subscribed to any streaming services. I just have plain cable. And I lost my remote a couple of weeks ago and haven't even taken the time to find it. I've been buried in books instead."

Mona said, "Maybe you should try one of the lower-priced tiers of service and see if you'll actually use it, then. I was skeptical at first because of the cost and because it was just . . . different from television. But Luna convinced me we should subscribe to Netflix at least. She said when we're watching cable, we're tied down to whatever is on the schedule. But with streaming, we can look up films and shows we actually would like to see and watch it on our own time."

Wilson nodded slowly. "She makes an excellent argument. I'll have to consider that. Thank you."

He headed away, but in the direction of the breakroom this time. I winked at Mona.

It was quiet enough that I was able to quickly knock out the column for Grayson. I handed it over to Wilson to glance over for typos or for general quality. He was still buried in research for how to spend Grace's donation. "It all looks good to me," he said with a bemused smile. "Don't worry about having me look at any of the other columns."

Which was a definite dismissal, but at least he liked the direction I'd gone in for the article. I supposed . . . it was hard to tell without feedback. I sent it along to Grayson and later received an enthusiastic email in return, so I'd apparently at least hit the note he was hoping for.

I was deep into the library calendar and looking for open dates for Wilson's volunteer appreciation day when I heard someone clearing his throat. I glanced up and saw Linus there.

I startled a little. "Linus! I'm so sorry, I forgot all about you." I glanced around, still thinking Wilson might be somehow lurking around to listen in as we discussed the contraband dog. "What's the update on the dog situation? Luna told me you'd been kind enough to buy a harness and leash for him. I can pay you back for that." I dug around on the shelf behind the circulation desk for my purse.

He quickly stopped my fumbling. "Please don't; I was happy to help out."

I straightened back up. "How is she? It is a she isn't it?"

He smiled at me. "She. And she seems to be doing well, although she doesn't have a microchip."

I frowned. "Oh, that's too bad. Well, we'll see if we get any response from the community. Maybe someone will realize she's their dog or will recognize her as their neighbor's. Luna put up some posters, didn't she?" I glanced around vaguely, the volunteer appreciation event still occupying my thoughts.

"Luna did. And she said she even put some notices up on the library's social media," said Linus.

"Well, with any luck, she'll be back with her family soon," I said in an upbeat tone. But I noticed a slight shadow cross Linus's face. Was he interested in this stray? "Where is she now? She couldn't be back outside the library or Wilson would be fussing about her."

Linus chuckled a little. "I figured that would be the way. The vet offered to hold onto her for a night or two. She said they had plenty of room in their kennels. She also said if we *didn't* find an owner that she would spay her and give her vaccinations for free."

I smiled again at the pleased expression on Linus's face, although I was surprised to see him have so much enthusiasm. He'd always been so quiet and stayed so emotionally level, no matter what chaos was going on in the library. I couldn't tell if Linus was interested in taking the dog home himself or not. I figured he'd offer up the information if he wanted to. He was such a private and quiet man that I didn't want to push him. "Well, thanks so much again for all our help. Luna and I will keep you updated on what we find out about a potential owner."

"And I'll keep you updated on the dog. I gave the vet my phone number as a contact." He hesitated. "Hope that was all right."

"More than all right," I said firmly. "It's very appreciated. Wilson would have been tearing his hair out if we were getting phone calls from the vet here all day."

He gave me a shy smile and disappeared into the stacks just as quickly as he'd appeared.

The next couple of days were gratifyingly normal. I worked, did some yardwork in my off-hours, and hung out with Fitz and a book at night. When I was at home, Luna called me on the phone. "Hey, I just found out Scott's funeral is tomorrow."

"I don't think I should attend, Luna. I didn't know him like the rest of you did. You all knew him from when you were growing up and I'd only just met him. And, honestly, not had the best of impressions."

"Of course you didn't! He was being vile. But I think we should go. Grace would probably be happy to see us there . . . you *know* she's going to attend. And if Grace is there, Wilson will want us to be there."

"What time is it?"

"It's at lunch. I've already asked Wilson about it and he urged us to go."

"Of course he did," I said wryly.

"And apparently, he's interviewing someone for a full-time position tomorrow, so we won't be as short-staffed soon as we have been."

I said, "He's moving quickly on that. I didn't think he'd get around to interviewing people for another couple of months. Especially since he's been trying to figure out how he wants to spend the new library windfall." I paused. "Okay, of course I'll go. I'll make sure to wear something suitably solemn tomorrow to work."

"I didn't even think about that. Ugh."

Luna's wardrobe was many things, but solemn wasn't one of them. You could definitely quickly find her in the library with her colorful, mismatched clothes. And the children in her section absolutely loved seeing the palette of color she displayed on a daily basis.

I said, "I know you have some black. I've seen you in it."

"I have a black, long-sleeved top that I wear with purple pants."

"And don't you have black slacks?"

"I do. That I usually wear with a chartreuse top," said Luna.

"Then just wear the black top and the black pants together."

The next morning at the library, Luna did look very solemn in her all-black ensemble. The morning passed quickly with a rush of patrons mid-morning. Then Luna drove us over to the cemetery where Scott's service was going to be held.

I was glad when we arrived that I'd come. There was just a small scattering of people there . . . mostly the other guests from the party.

Luna said in a low voice, "Scott's mother and his brother are over there. I recognize them from years ago."

"They don't still live here?"

"No. They're in other states, although I can't remember which ones. Wow, I'm glad we're here. You'd expect to see more people here, especially with a funeral for a younger person." Luna grimaced.

We hung near the back of the group. Grace gave us an acknowledging smile. Kyle was there, shifting awkwardly from time to time and looking uncomfortable. He paid close attention as another car approached and Felicity got out and walked over. A few minutes later, Roz and Kelly arrived. Roz's face was solemn and Kelly's eyes were red from crying.

The service was fairly short. The minister read some Bible verses, we sang a fairly somber hymn, and there were no eulogies. Perhaps the family didn't want them or perhaps no one had wanted to give them. As soon as the service was over, we joined a line of others to speak with Scott's brother and mother.

Kyle stood next to us as we waited. Luna murmured, "I feel so bad for his family. His brother looks wrecked."

He did. He must have been a little younger than Scott, but looked so much like him it was almost eerie. He was very pale and looked as though he was going to need to sit down at any time.

Kyle nodded. "And now they're going to have to settle his debts. And they've never had much money, themselves."

"Debts?" Luna stared at him. "But Scott made all that money with his dot-com."

Kyle looked sad for a split second at the mention of the business. Then he quickly said, "He did. He made a ton of money. But Scott also *spent* a ton of money. And he was remarkably bad at investments for somebody with a decent head for business."

He quickly stopped speaking as it was his turn to speak with the family. Luna and I shared a look at the news of Scott's finances.

When we'd given the family our condolences, Scott's brother said to us, "We're inviting everyone here today to go to the café downtown for a bite to eat with us. They have a private room at the back that they've set up for us and they'll have some sandwiches and drinks. Just a modest spread. We wanted to have a funeral reception, but being from out of town, it's hard."

I hesitated, feeling a bit like a fraud for having these folks spend money on my lunch, especially since I didn't know Scott well and hadn't even particularly liked what I'd seen of him. But Luna quickly accepted for the both of us.

Chapter Thirteen

Ten minutes later, we were back in Luna's car and following the others to downtown Whitby.

"Hope you don't mind," said Luna. "I just felt bad that there aren't more people here."

I said, "No, I agree. I just hate for them to have to pay for my lunch, especially from what Kyle was saying."

"But they've already ordered the food and it's going to be out there whether you're in attendance or not. Besides, we haven't had time to eat, ourselves," said Luna reasonably.

We parked the car and followed everyone inside and to the back room of the small café where there were tables and chairs and a buffet with a variety of sandwiches, potato salad, fruit, chips, and drinks.

We helped our plates and then sat down at one of the tables. Felicity spotted us and sat down with us as Kyle looked disappointed about missing his opportunity.

She gave us a smile and said in a low voice, "It's nice of you two to be here. I don't think Scott knew many people here and of course his family's friends live out of town. I'm glad they let you leave work for his service."

Luna said, "We wanted to come." She glanced at me. "I didn't think about it before, but maybe this is a little bit of closure for us, in a way."

I didn't think there would really be any closure until Scott's murderer was caught and the police wrapped up the investigation. Technically, we were all suspects. I didn't think Burton seriously considered Luna or me to be viable candidates for Scott's murder, but we had to be suspects, just the same.

Felicity nodded. "I know what you mean. What a weekend." She blew out a sigh, looked down at her plate of food and pushed it slightly away. "I don't think I can even eat a bite. I'm not sure why I even got food. My stomach has been in knots since I left Grace's house. I don't know what Grace was thinking, putting that particular group together. It was a recipe for disaster."

I said, "She must have originally thought she was doing the right thing. After all, Kelly would have wanted Scott to be there. And she seemed to think it would be nice for your group to catch up with each other."

"Was it though?" asked Felicity wryly. "It didn't work at all."

"You were all close growing up, though, weren't you?" I asked.

"Well, sure. But it's a different time, isn't it? And here in Whitby, you have a very limited body of people to choose to be friends with. If we'd all gone to school in a bigger town, maybe we'd never have even chosen each other as company. Besides, I don't think we *needed* a reunion. I mean, it was nice to see Grace. She's the one we haven't seen for a while. But it wasn't as

if we had this lovely, idyllic time when we were in high school."
She grimaced.

I asked, "Is Grace the same as she was in high school? She's
just so confident now and it's hard to imagine high schoolers being that self-assured."

Felicity shook her head. Lowering her voice she said, "Money can do that for you. Grace was a very different person in high
school. Very socially-awkward. Quiet. She followed our group
around and just kind of inserted herself. And she seemed to have
the biggest crush on Scott. Whenever he was around, she'd just
gape at him."

Lula snorted. "I'm sure he ate that up. He had the ego for it."

"He did. He wasn't going out with anyone at the time, but
he clearly wasn't interested in Grace, although he'd joke around
with her some. It was an unrequited love on Grace's part," said
Felicity.

Luna said, "Scott was a mess, but I feel bad for him. He
didn't deserve what happened to him."

Felicity said, "That's the second time I've known someone
who's drowned. I may never swim again. And I do feel badly . . .
especially for Scott's mother and brother. This must have been a
devastating shock for them."

I noticed Felicity didn't seem to suffer from the heavy sense
of guilt some of the other guests had felt. I wanted to find out
what *she* was doing around the time Scott died so I offered my
own alibi. "I just wish I could have done something to help. It
gives me this sort of helpless feeling to know I wasn't far away
and could have maybe stopped this. Instead, I fell into a really
sound sleep. Too much sun and too much wine, I suppose."

Luna glanced over at me and I could tell she understood what I was trying to do. She stayed quiet and Felicity said, "I know what you mean. Part of me knows Scott was on a path of self-destruction that night, but somebody decided to help him on his way. I wasn't any help at all, of course. I could hear loud music still playing in the pool room and I could hear it all the way in my room. I thought about going down there and asking everyone to turn the music down, but I didn't want to deal with Scott again so I just plugged my ears up with my earbuds and played some soft music. I didn't hear a thing from downstairs."

Luna blurted out, "So what do you think, Felicity?" She whispered, "Who did this? The police think it was someone at the party."

Felicity shook her head. "I'm totally in the dark. I can't believe any of us could have done it. But let's face it—he made everybody mad. Well, not the two of you, although his attitude probably annoyed you to death. But everybody else was totally done with him. Technically, any one of us could have done it. The only way I can make sense of it all is that it must have been completely unplanned. Someone got fed up, lashed out impetuously at Scott in anger, and then were probably shocked at what they did and are lying to cover it up."

I said hesitantly, "There was one thing I wanted to ask you about, Felicity. I overheard Scott and Kelly at one point over the weekend and Scott was saying there was something he needed to talk to you about."

Felicity nodded. "He asked me for the name of a good tax lawyer. He figured I might be connected to some through my job or at least have heard of some."

Luna made a face. "That doesn't sound good."

Felicity shrugged. "It sounded like he needed some help with his business. I told him I'd send him the name of someone, but then . . . well, I didn't end up needing to."

She stopped as Kyle pulled up a chair and sat down with them.

Felicity said, "How is Scott's family holding up? I saw you've been speaking with them."

Kyle shook his head. "They're really shaken. I feel awful for them. They did ask me if I could lend them a hand with Scott's things. I told them of course I'd help out."

"That's nice of you," said Luna. "I didn't even think about that. It would be tough for them, especially living in another state."

Kyle nodded. "I feel like I should be able to help them more, but at least this is a start."

He turned and said to me, "By the way, thanks again, Ann, for the book club information. I'm hoping to make the next meeting."

Felicity raised her eyebrows. "I didn't realize you were interested in the book club. I could have filled you in, myself. Ann gave me all kinds of information on it."

Kyle flushed a little. "Oh, I overheard you and Ann talking about it last weekend and thought I might want to check it out."

"I'd gotten the impression you were a big reader already," said Felicity. "I'm surprised you can find time to fit it in."

Kyle's eyes crinkled in a smile. "I'm a big reader, for sure. The problem is that I always find myself picking out the same types of books. I've been thinking about joining a book club for a while, hoping I could broaden my list and fit in some other genres. I don't read a lot of nonfiction. This club sounded right up my alley."

The rest of the lunch was spent talking amiably about books and other things before Luna and I once again spoke to the family, and spent the rest of our day busily engaged at the library.

That night, I was curled up in bed with Fitz snuggled against me when my phone rang. There's nothing quite as jarring as an incoming phone call at 3:30 a.m.

I answered it, my voice hoarse and alarmed.

It was Luna. "Ann, it's me. Roz is dead."

Chapter Fourteen

I went from dead asleep to wide awake in a matter of seconds. "What happened?" I put the phone on speaker, swung my legs off the bed, and was already changing out of my pjs.

Luna's voice shook. "Burton came by. He said she'd been murdered. She was found on the stairs at her apartment building. She was hit on the back of the head."

I put shoes on and glanced again at my clock. "She was on her way to work?"

"That's right. She had a 3 a.m. to 3 p.m. shift. Can you come by? We could use a steadying influence here—Mom's in a state and I'm not much better. I'm sorry to ask you to do this."

"Of course I'll be there," I said. I'd automatically started changing into work clothes, even though it would be hours before we had to be at work, just in case.

A few minutes later, after feeding Fitz and giving him an apologetic rub, I arrived at Luna and Mona's house. The lights were all on in the house, standing out in stark contrast the rest of the dark street.

Mona was wearing a long robe and slippers and her eyes were red as she gave me a quick hug for coming over. Luna had apparently gone ahead and dressed for the day and looked grimly at me.

"I'll make you some coffee," said Mona briskly, ignoring my protests.

Luna waved a tired hand at me. "She doesn't want to hear the recap again. Who can blame her?"

"What happened?" I asked quietly as Mona busied herself in the next room.

"We don't know much. Burton was so thoughtful to come by and deliver the news before we heard it from anyone else. He knew Roz and I were cousins." Luna grimaced. "Mom insists on calling her sister herself later. Thinks it's her responsibility. It's going to be awful."

I said, "So Roz was on her way to work. And it sounds as if someone was waiting to when she left. But it wasn't a robbery?"

Luna shook her head. "No one touched her purse or took her phone." She took a deep breath. "Somebody from this weekend did this, Ann. One of Roz's friends. There's no other explanation."

I said, "Did you get the sense Roz knew something? Did she say anything to you?"

Luna sighed. "She didn't say a word. I wish she had. But I did feel like she was holding something back. Roz looked worried."

"Where was her room situated? You went by there, didn't you?"

Luna said, "Yeah, I stopped by her room and visited a couple of times when I was just walking past. She had a perfect view of the pool room." She made a face.

"So Roz could have seen something. Maybe she spotted something that at first didn't even seem like a problem. But then she could have realized someone's alibi or story wasn't completely accurate."

Luna sighed. "And the problem is that Roz was the kind of person who would have just gone right ahead and confronted the person with whatever information she had. Of course she *should* have gone right to Burton. But that wouldn't have been Roz's usual m.o. She was always really upfront."

Luna's phone started ringing and she frowned. "It's not time to go to the library, is it?"

"Not even close."

She fished out her phone from the depths of a pocket and frowned at it. "Kelly?" she asked as she answered it.

I could hear sobbing on the other end of the phone line and saw Luna frown again as she tried to figure out what Kelly was saying. She shrugged at me and shook her head, unable to make it out.

"Kelly? Kelly. Look, we're going to come over there to be with you, okay? Ann's here, too and we're on our way." She paused for a moment to allow more indecipherable words to be said and then continued, "Right. We'll be right there." She hung up and gave me a look. "Well, obviously, Kelly isn't taking the news of Roz's death very well." She called out to her mom to make sure she was going to be all right and Mona waved her on.

I said, "I can drive us over there if you direct me." Luna wasn't a great driver under ordinary circumstances and these were far from ordinary.

A few minutes later and after making a couple of wrong turns along the way, Luna and I were knocking at Kelly's front door. She lived in a cozy Cape Cod house with a perfectly-trimmed yard and a lush hedge around the house.

The door flew open and a haggard Kelly stood there. She gave us both a hug and led us inside her tidy home. The only signs of anything awry were with Kelly herself. Her hair was sticking up around her head and she was wearing a bathrobe and slippers. Her eyes were swollen from crying but I noted she'd calmed herself down a little as we'd made our way over here.

"Thank you so much for coming over," she said fervently as we sat down in her living room. "I don't think I could be alone right now. My mind is racing around in circles. I feel so bad for Roz." Her voice broke again.

Luna reaching over and clumsily patted her hand. "We all do. But from what the police told me, Roz's death must have been almost instant. She didn't really have a chance to even register what happened."

"I'm so glad. But there must still have been a few seconds when she felt herself being pushed." Kelly shuddered and then clamped her lips shut. A few moments later she added, "I'm so sorry, Luna. She was your cousin. You're right—the police said her death was practically instantaneous. I just feel so helpless. I was here, sleeping, when she was battling for her life."

I said, "It seems unbelievable, doesn't it?"

Kelly nodded. "It does." She hesitated. "But I did have an inkling something might be wrong. I didn't think it would be something *this* wrong. But I sent Roz a couple of text messages last night and she didn't respond to them. She's always really good about responding to text messages."

Luna frowned. "But she didn't fall until the middle of the night. When did you text her?"

"Oh, Roz always turned in super-early. Maybe eight o'clock on nights she was working. So I'd send her a text and she'd reply in the middle of the night while I was sleeping. I'd continue the thread after I woke up in the morning and she'd respond when she took a break. That was sort of our routine." Kelly stopped short as if realizing this was another thing that wasn't going to be continuing any longer.

I said quietly, "So it was really unusual for Roz not to write back. When did you realize she hadn't? Were you up some last night, too?"

"Actually, I was. I woke up at three o'clock to use the restroom and glanced at my phone then. Usually Roz would have already responded by then, so I was surprised. But I figured maybe something had come up at the hospital and she was too focused on getting to work to reply." Kelly sighed. "I tried to get back to sleep, but I kept thinking how weird it was. I ended up calling the hospital to see if Roz had made it there okay. They told me she hadn't come in."

Luna glanced over at me and then said to Kelly, "I thought you'd found out about Roz from the police."

Kelly shook her head. "I knew something was up when the hospital told me she hadn't come in. I drove over to her apartment and that's when I talked to the police. They were already all over the place there."

I said, "I wonder how they knew to come."

Kelly gave a shuddering breath. "They told me a neighbor heard a loud noise on the stairs outside her apartment. She stuck her head out to see what it was and then called the police." She stopped for a few moments and said, "This had to be someone from the party. There's no other way. Roz wasn't robbed. She was silenced."

Luna glanced at me again. I said, "Did she say anything to you about hearing or seeing something at the party? Something to do with Scott's death?"

Kelly gave her a dull look and groaned. "She said something after we'd gotten back home from Grace's house. But she didn't really tell me what it was that she'd seen. She only said she was worried about something she saw the night Scott died."

Luna frowned. "Did you ask her what she meant by that?"

Kelly covered her eyes. "No. I didn't. Now I feel so stupid for not being a good listener. I was still reeling from Scott's death. He and I really had something special together." She uncovered her eyes and must have seen Luna and I looking skeptical because she quickly added, "I know what it must have looked like over the weekend. Believe me, I feel really ashamed of how I was acting. I was reacting way too much to everything Scott was saying instead of just letting it wash over me. But deep down, he and I had a really remarkable relationship. We'd known each other for so long that I knew what he was thinking and vice-versa. I could finish his sentences for him. No matter how many rough patches our relationship went through, we always had that special connection."

I said, "You're really lucky to have had a relationship like that." Kelly perked up at this and beamed at me. I cautiously continued, "So Roz didn't really explain what she meant by being worried about something she'd seen?"

Kelly's expression clouded again and she shook her head. "She didn't. And I feel terrible for not asking her about it. Like I said, I was too wrapped up in grief over Scott's death. I just know Roz wasn't entirely sure she could trust her own eyes."

I said, "She said that?"

Kelly nodded. "She was really hesitant about saying anything because she said she'd been drinking so much champagne after we got back from the club, she wasn't really sure how accurate what she'd seen was. Or the timing of it." She paused and then sighed. "Considering what happened, I'm guessing she saw something really damaging. She must have seen somebody down at the pool with Scott. Maybe somebody who'd said they'd already gone to bed for the night."

I said, "You know everybody who was at the party really well. What do you think happened to Roz?"

Kelly said sadly, "I think she probably called or spoke in person to whoever she thought she'd seen with Scott. After all, her room had a clear view of the pool. She wouldn't have wanted to tell the police if she wasn't really sure she'd seen something suspicious. Roz would have contacted the person to clear it up—'hey, I know you said you'd already turned in, but I think I saw you down at the pool again.' She'd have wanted to clear it all up."

Luna rubbed her forehead as if it hurt. "I just don't get how somebody knew to lie in wait for her like that. I mean, were they there all night, waiting for her to go to work? Wouldn't that have been really dangerous? One of the other apartment residents could have seen whoever it was."

Kelly gave her a rueful look. "I don't think the person did that at all. Remember how we were all talking about work over dinner? You and Luna talked a little about the library and then Roz talked about her schedule and when she leaves for work—just because it was so freaking early that it was a point of interest to everyone. So the whole table heard her routine and when she left for work. Whoever did this could have easily parked their car, gone up to her apartment, and waited in the shadows for her to come out."

I said slowly, "Who might have been capable of something like that?"

Kelly gave another harsh laugh. "I'd have said *nobody* I know was capable of that, but now I know differently. After all, somebody already killed Scott and now they've killed Roz. Someone is a lot more dangerous than I ever realized. But like I already told the police, I don't *know* anything. I didn't see or hear anything. I can just guess as to who might have done it."

Luna put her hands on her hips as if squaring herself for battle. "And who comes to mind?"

Kelly shrugged and then sighed. "I don't know if you've heard about this, but the police have been talking to me. They know I came back to the party the night Scott died."

I carefully made sure my face was blank. Kyle hadn't told Burton about this, but clearly somebody else had seen Kelly return. Kelly continued, "I know that sounds bad. I'm not sure if either of you were awake when I came back in."

I said ruefully, "I slept pretty soundly that night."

"Me too," said Luna. "All the alcohol knocked me out, I guess. I'm just not used to it."

Kelly said, "I'm not sure who told the police about me coming back, but I'm guessing it was Kyle."

"What makes you think that?" I asked. I knew it wasn't Kyle, but I did want to hear Kelly's opinion of him.

Kelly blew out a gusty sigh. "Nothing, really. I mean, I've known Kyle for a zillion years. Like I said before, I can't really imagine any of my friends getting rid of Scott. But let's face it—Kyle was really annoyed with Scott and it wasn't just because of his behavior over the weekend, either."

Luna said, "I heard something about Kyle and Scott falling out over business stuff."

Kelly said, "Not *really*. I mean, they didn't really fall out. I think Kyle can be something of a pushover and he didn't really protest when Scott took over the company Kyle helped found and develop. Scott bragged to me that he'd undercut Kyle and hadn't really compensated him properly for his part." She shrugged. "He thought it made him a shrewd businessman."

I frowned. "But they didn't argue over that?"

Kelly shook her head. "Nope. Kyle continued still hanging out with Scott. I even brought up to Kyle privately one time that I'd heard he should have done better when Scott bought him out. But Kyle defended him." She shrugged. "That's the way he's always been. But I wonder if this weekend was the final straw for him."

Luna said, "You mean because Scott was hitting on Felicity?"

"Exactly. Scott, of all people, knew Kyle had always carried a torch for Felicity, ever since we were kids. I mean, Kyle did see someone else for a while in high school, but then he was back to mooning after Felicity not long afterward. Not that Felicity is paying attention enough to realize that." Kelly snorted. "Her mind is always somewhere else. Maybe business, these days. Anyway, I could see Kyle's blood pressure going up every time Scott sat next to her or talked to her."

Luna said, "And yours too, right? I mean, that was your boyfriend acting that way."

Kelly said, "But it wasn't unusual behavior for Scott and it didn't mean anything. He was just trying to get under my skin, that's all. Kyle might have seen it differently, though."

I said, "And I'm guessing you think he's responsible for telling the police you came back to the house?"

"I don't really know *what* to think. But I could see Kyle telling the police for a few reasons. For one, he's the kind of guy who could possibly fold under pressure. If the police were really pressing him for information, I can see him blurting it right out, even though he knows, of all people, that I'm the last person who'd have killed Scott. Besides, if he saw me arriving, he probably saw me leaving, too. I stormed back out of there just a few minutes later."

"Why *did* you come back?" asked Luna. "Did you forget something at the house?"

Kelly gave a dry laugh. "Scott texted me to break up with me. Can you believe it?"

"What?" Luna asked, eyes bulging. It still totally sounded to me like something a middle school kid would do to his first girlfriend.

"That's what I said. I wasn't going to let that pass with a texted reply, believe me. I hopped back in the car and drove as fast as I could back over to Grace's house. I stormed to the pool, figuring he was still there and sure enough, there he was." A mixture of pain and residual anger were in Kelly's eyes.

I said, "What did Scott say?"

"Nothing. Actually, he kind of looked surprised." Kelly shrugged. "Maybe he thought I'd take that lying down and just let the relationship end and was surprised that I'd come back over. Maybe he was just shocked to see how mad I really was. I mean, he'd seen me angry plenty of times, right? The two of you saw me angry with him last weekend. But I really saw red this time."

"What happened?" breathed Luna as if half-expecting Kelly to say she whacked Scott over the head with the champagne bottle.

"Like I said, Scott didn't say a word. I ranted at him for three or four minutes straight, telling him he needed to treat me better and stop acting like a spoiled brat. Then I told him under no circumstance would I consider our relationship over and done with—not while he was that drunk and not via text message. He opened and closed his mouth a few times and then watched me stomp back out of the pool room and head for the driveway."

"So he was alive when you saw him," said Luna.

"That's right. And no, initially I *didn't* want to tell the cops I'd gone back to Grace's house after I'd left. Can you blame me?

Scott and I had been fighting all weekend and then he suddenly ended up dead—apparently right after I'd returned to Grace's house. I was going to be their top suspect." She gave a dry laugh. "I probably am, anyway. But yes, he was totally alive when I saw him. Not just alive but in the pool and trying to swim. If I hadn't heard he was murdered, I'd have just assumed he'd drowned . . . he wasn't being really coordinated after all he'd drunk." The last words came out in a sob.

Luna reached out and gave Kelly a hug and Kelly struggled to regain control. "I just hate that the last time I saw him, we were arguing with each other. I don't know if I'll ever get over that. At least Roz and I always got along really well. I don't know what I'd do if she and I had been on bad terms before she died."

Luna said, "You two always seemed to get along so well."

"We never had cross words between us," said Kelly. She looked at her watch. "I'm sorry. Luna, you've just lost your cousin and here I am needing all the support. And the two of you have got to get ready for work. Thanks so much for coming over . . . I think I'm okay now."

"Are you sure?" asked Luna, peering at her as if there might be tell-tale signs on Kelly's face.

"I am. I'm just going to make a pot of coffee, take a long shower, and get ready for my day," she said firmly.

"You won't take the day off?" I asked.

"No, I need the distraction. I really need some normalcy, period. I feel like I've stepped through the Looking Glass or something. I want a regular day."

So Luna promised to check in on Kelly later and she and I headed out.

Chapter Fifteen

"Thanks for going over there with me," said Luna as I drove away from Kelly's house. She gave me a sideways glance. "What did you make of all that?"

I sighed. "Well, she did come right out and admit she was back over at Grace's house. Kyle had already told me that after film club yesterday."

Luna said, "So I guess Kyle probably told the police about Kelly. Do you think Kelly's right? Kyle told the cops to deflect attention from himself?"

"I don't think he said anything about it. It must have been somebody else. He was adamant he didn't want to tell the police about Kelly returning to the party."

"Okay. Although it really sounds like Scott cheated Kyle out of the money he deserved when he bought him out," said Luna, frowning.

"Does that sound like Scott?"

"It sure does. He was always kind of sly with money that way. I remember back in high school, he had a reputation as a card shark. He'd play poker on the weekends and made a lot of money."

I said, "But it sounded like Kyle wasn't even that upset about getting the short end of the stick when Scott bought him out. It sounded like he might have been more upset over the way Scott was paying attention to Felicity."

"Yeah. But he shouldn't have. It was pretty obvious to me that Scott was only doing it to get under Kelly's skin. Every time he sat down next to Felicity or started a conversation with her, he always glanced over at Kelly to see what her reaction was."

I said, "But maybe Kyle saw it as a betrayal. Did you remember him always having a crush on Felicity?"

Luna snorted. "Everybody knew that. For ages."

"Except Felicity?"

"There are none so blind as those who will not see," quoted Luna loftily.

I hesitated and then asked quietly, "Can I ask you something about Roz?"

Luna glanced over at me. "Sure."

"Grace mentioned being worried about her drinking. She said something about Roz packing her own alcohol for the party."

"What?" Luna snorted. "No way. Why would Grace say that?"

I shook my head. "I don't have any idea. She seemed to believe it, though."

"Maybe Roz just brought some extra alcohol along to contribute to the party in case Grace got low. Not that it was needed. Anyway, no, Roz didn't have a drinking problem. Did she drink too much the night Scott died? Definitely. I saw her slug down those two glasses of champagne. But she was just blowing off stress. That definitely wasn't a normal thing for her."

I dropped Luna by her house and then headed home so I could do a few things before going to the library. My head was spinning and I needed to focus before work. Once I got home, Fitz came immediately over to love on me as if he could sense I needed comfort. I sat down with him and a cup of Irish breakfast tea on the sofa and softly stroked him for about thirty minutes while he purred loudly. Then I ran a brush through my hair, touched up my makeup, and Fitz and I left for the library.

Unfortunately, it wasn't a busy enough morning to distract me much from my thoughts and it seemed to be quiet in the children's area, too. I kept busy by shelving books and putting requested books on the hold shelf. I did have one research request that kept me occupied for about forty minutes—a deep-dive finding information on a patron's mother's medical issue. But still the minutes crept by.

At eleven o'clock, the library door swung open and I was surprised to see Grace Armstrong standing there. Well, surprised and not at the same time. I wasn't really expecting her to drop by the library, but it made sense that she'd try to get in contact with Luna or me about Roz's death. She'd want to find out more information about what happened and she'd have realized we were probably at work.

Wilson, who seemed to always have some sort of radar when it came to library trustees or, apparently, donors immediately popped out of his office. He straightened his already-perfectly-straight tie as he strode over.

"It's so good to see you," he said smoothly, holding his hand out to Grace.

She smiled at him and shook his hand.

"Ann and Luna said you received a tour the last time you were here. Would you be interested in hearing some of the ideas I have for using your kind donation?" asked Wilson.

Grace seemed to be an expert at politely bypassing things she didn't want to do. "You know, that sounds like a great idea, but I'd like to do it another time, if that's all right with you. I was just dropping by to see if Ann and Luna were available for lunch again."

"Both of us?" I asked. It was already unprecedented that Luna and I had both been away from the library simultaneously for the weekend party, the lunch, and Scott's funeral. Ordinarily, the library would want to have either the children's librarian or me available.

A crease of irritation appeared between Wilson's eyebrows as he looked reprovingly at me. "Certainly, both of you, if that's what Grace wants."

I was trying to adjust to this new, alternate reality as Grace said quickly, "Of course, if it's not convenient . . ."

"It's *more* than convenient. After all, it's been a very quiet day here at the library. Enjoy your lunch, Ann. Take as long as you need. I'll let Luna know." Then, straightening his tie one last, unnecessary time, he hurried off to the children's section.

Grace chuckled. "Why do I get the feeling that you and Luna don't usually have lunch together?"

I said dryly, "Because it's completely unheard of, as you've guessed."

"I seem to be wielding a lot of power here," said Grace with a smile. "It wasn't even *that* big of a donation."

"It doesn't take much," I said. But I was aware of the size of Grace's donation. If she didn't think it was a large one, she was even wealthier than I'd thought.

Luna hurried up. "Lunch?" she breathlessly asked.

Grace's face turned solemn. "Yes. And Luna, I'm so sorry about Roz. I wanted to check in with both of you and I figured lunch was the best way to do it. Should we go somewhere different this time?"

Remembering the huge amount of food we'd gotten last time, I nodded. I was also going to try to pay for my own meal this time. "There's a vegan deli that's down the street that's really good, if you're not familiar with it. And there's always Quittin' Time," I added in a wry voice. I didn't think Quittin' Time was probably up Grace's alley, but the deli might be.

As I'd expected, she immediately latched onto the idea of eating vegan. "It was actually one of my resolutions this year to try to have more veggie days. Let's try the deli."

I was a little worried that Luna might confront Grace about the fact she'd told me Roz was packing her own alcohol for the party. Luna read my mind and whispered, "Don't worry. I won't say a thing."

I was glad that (after a few protests), Grace let Luna and me pay for our own food. I never really like to be beholden to people and was starting to get that uncomfortable feeling with Grace. I ordered a veggie burger and a side of sweet potato fries and Luna and Grace both got the portabella wrap with grilled vegetables on the side.

When we were halfway through our meal, Grace turned somber again. "Luna, once again, I'm so sorry about your cousin. Did you find out any information from the police as to what they think happened? Or who they might be looking for? It just seems completely unbelievable that this has happened again."

Luna said, "I just know that it wasn't an accident—that Roz was murdered. They didn't say anything about who they were looking for. I guess most people won't have much of an alibi since it happened in the middle of the night. We'll all say we were asleep in our beds."

Grace nodded. "Ironically, last night was one of the only good nights of sleep I've had since Scott died. I'm usually tossing and turning like crazy in my bed every night. Then, when I *do* sleep, I have these really awful nightmares. But last night I slept like a baby. Then I was getting ready for work when the police came by."

Luna's eyes were huge. "The police came by to talk to *you*? Why?"

"I'm guessing they're going to talk to everyone who was at my party last weekend. And who can blame them? This isn't exactly a town with a big crime problem. It's normal for them to look for a connection." Grace shook her head. "I can see somebody getting mad enough at Scott to murder him. But *Roz*? What on earth could anybody have had against Roz?"

We sat quietly for a few moments and I said carefully, "Like you, I have a hard time thinking someone was upset directly at Roz. I'm wondering if maybe Roz saw or heard something the night Scott died and maybe that's the reason someone came after her."

"What a terrible world we live in," said Grace. "Roz didn't say anything to me about seeing something. Did she say anything to either of you?"

I shook my head and so did Luna.

Grace sighed. "Maybe it's one of those things where we'll never know what really happened. That seems like a reasonable guess, though, Ann. Believe it or not, it makes me feel a little better. I hated thinking that someone—someone I *knew*—would do something so senseless."

Luna said, "I wish it made me feel better. I'm still sort of numb."

Grace gave her a sympathetic look. "I'm surprised you made it to work today. Is Wilson that bad to work for?"

Luna shook her head. "I'm sure he'd have let me take the day off. But the truth of the matter is that if I'd have stayed home with my mom, I'd have probably ended up thinking about Roz all day and feeling sad. At least at work I'm distracted. I don't have as much time to just sit around and think. I mean, it could be busier at the library today, but it's still better than being at home."

Grace grimaced. "And here I am making you talk about it. Sorry, that was pretty thoughtless of me."

"No, I don't mind. It would be weird not to talk about it at all. It would be like I was ignoring Roz or trying to put her out of my head." She frowned. "Anyway, I want to find out who did this. I mean, it was upsetting when Scott died at your party, Grace. But this was *Roz*. Did you give the police any direction at all when you talked to them? Who do you think might have done this?" asked Luna.

Grace hesitated and then said cautiously, "Well, I didn't really tell them anything because I don't know anything. It's just me guessing and guessing doesn't seem really fair. It's like I'm pointing a finger for no real reason."

Luna said with a touch of impatience in her voice, "But who are you thinking of when you're making your guesses? It's just Ann and me."

Grace paused again and then reluctantly said, "I mentioned Kyle to them. But I felt bad doing it. I was with both of them a couple of weeks ago at lunch and Kyle blew up at Scott out of the clear blue."

I asked, "Blew up at him?"

She nodded. "He was ranting like I've never heard him do before. Kyle is always so measured with everything he says and does. And Scott hasn't always been the best friend to Kyle, but Kyle has never said a word against him. And if somebody else says something bad about Scott, Kyle always has stepped in and defended him."

Luna said, "What kinds of things was Kyle saying?"

Grace gave a short laugh. "I was trying so hard to just disappear that I don't think I even listened to half of it. But it was what I'd have *thought* he'd rant about. The fact that Scott wasn't fair to him when he bought him out. Stuff like that. He really lost it."

"That must have made for a really uncomfortable lunch," I said.

Grace shrugged. "Just as soon as it started, it was over. And Kyle seemed completely deflated like there wasn't an ounce of anger left in him anymore. It just made me wonder if maybe he was capable of lashing out at Scott again. After all, I don't think what happened to Scott was *planned*, right? It was just somebody who'd had too much to drink, wasn't thinking clearly, and got really upset with Scott. And, let's face it: Scott was in a frame of mind to make people upset." She shook her head. "Once again, I'm really sorry I put that group of people together. It's amazing how well we all got on when we were young." She laughed, a little bitterly. "You won't believe it, but I used to have the biggest crush on Scott in high school."

Luna said, "People change though, and not always in good ways. Scott was obviously a different person."

Conversation switched to lighter topics then as we finished up our lunch and Grace took us back to the library.

Luna headed to the children's section to get ready for her preschool storytime and I headed for the periodical area, remembering one thing I needed to follow up on.

When I approached Linus, he politely stood up from his armchair, carefully placing a bookmark in the biography he was reading.

I gave him a reassuring smile since he looked just slightly anxious. "Hey there, Linus. Just wanted to let you know that despite the posters and the social media posts and the things we've put on online lost-and-found pet forums, there has been no response. Just people asking if the dog was up for adoption."

He breathed out slightly as if he'd been holding his breath. "She's a sweet-looking dog," he said. "I'm not too surprised people are wanting to adopt her. But no one is an owner?"

I shook my head. "And I think we've done our due diligence, especially in a town this size. Someone would have known if it was their neighbor's pet or their friend's. Have you heard anything from the vet?"

His eyes twinkled. "Apparently, they love her there. They've been keeping her with them behind the front desk and she's been helping to greet the furry patients."

"I think you can go ahead and let the vet know she's welcome to do the vaccinations and to fix her," I said. I hesitated and asked gently, "Did you have any ideas for a good home for her?"

He glanced away and then back at me. "Actually, I thought I might consider adopting her myself."

I smiled encouragingly at him. "Luna mentioned that you seemed to have a great connection with the dog."

He smiled tentatively back. "She reminds me very much of a favorite pet I had when I was ten years old. I loved that dog. After school, I spent all my time with her, running through the woods, playing in the creek. I'd build forts and dam up the creek to make swimming holes. It was great fun."

I wondered again about Linus and his seemingly solitary life—it appeared he'd also been something of a loner when he was a child, too. But he'd had such a good relationship with his wife, apparently. Maybe she'd been an introvert, too.

I said, "That sounds like a great plan. Let me know how she does at the vet. Did you think of a name for her?"

"Do you think it would be odd to name her after my child-hood dog?" he asked hesitantly.

"I think it would be a wonderful tribute," I said.

"Then I'll call her Ivy," he said with a smile. He grew solemn for a minute. "Luna told me about the death at the house party. And about her cousin."

Luna's way of feeling better about things was definitely talk therapy. I tended to clam up and keep my worries to myself. I knew Luna's way was probably a lot healthier. I nodded. "Their deaths were real tragedies."

Linus cleared his throat and said softly, "I don't think it was the first time they've encountered tragedy, either."

"It's not? I'm sorry—I didn't know you knew them."

Linus shook his head. "I didn't. And, of course, I wasn't living here when it happened. But I overheard Roz speaking with Luna about something that happened when Roz and her friends were teenagers." He blushed a little. "Roz's voice carried a bit."

This was true. And Luna wasn't exactly quiet, either.

"Did Roz say what the tragedy was?" I asked.

"No, only that someone had died. This was before you and Luna went on the weekend—I guess Roz they were talking about the people who were going. I only remember because Roz got very serious . . . actually, she seemed to choke up."

He briskly said, "I should let you get back to work. Hope things start looking up for you, Ann."

The library remained quiet the rest of the day, but I was glad because it gave me the opportunity to catch up on a lot of things I hadn't had a chance to work on. I spent some time looking up how other libraries held volunteer appreciation days and jotted down their tips. Then I constructed a loose agenda for the day . . . a date I still needed to pass by Wilson. I decided to go ahead and see if I could get approval from him for everything I'd put together.

Wilson looked up and smiled distractedly as I tapped on his office door.

"How did lunch go, Ann?" He pushed aside a pile of papers on his desk and leaned forward, suddenly regaining focus.

"It was good," I said cautiously. I wasn't sure what Wilson expected me to do during these lunches. I thought it might be good enough to be a good representative of the library, but I was starting to wonder if he thought I should be singing the library's praises or trying to ask for a recurring gift or something of that nature.

A moment later, it seemed his thoughts *were* going in that direction when he said, "Did Grace say anything about the library or how she might want to be involved in it in the future? Do you think she might be interested in a position on the board of trustees?"

I shook my head. "I'm sorry Wilson, but it wasn't that kind of lunch. In fact, I should have mentioned this to you this morning, but I got caught up with a bunch of things in my inbox. Luna's cousin, a friend of Grace's, died early this morning. I think Grace wanted to talk about it with us over lunch and that's why she invited us out."

Wilson's face reflected momentary disappointment before he said, "Of course. I'm sorry to hear about Luna's cousin." He frowned. "I'm surprised she came in today."

"I was too, but she said it would make for a good distraction for her. She and her mother were very upset this morning."

Wilson's frown deepened. "Her mother, yes. Mona. She was kind to make us all Rice Krispy treats the other day."

I said with a slightly pointed edge in my voice, "I believe she got the idea because you'd mentioned you liked them. She made them mostly for you."

Wilson suddenly seemed flustered, pulling the piles of paperwork closer to him as if needing to run interference between himself and my words. "Yes, well. That was *especially* nice, then." He hesitated and then asked, "Did she do that for any specific reason? That you know of anyway? I haven't been sure about how to behave around her. After all, she's the mother of an employee of mine."

I said simply, "She made them because she likes you. She hoped you'd enjoy them."

Wilson nodded slowly. "I should do something in return, then. Especially since she's going through this rough time with the death of her niece." He considered this. "Perhaps a card."

I was able not to wince. I was hoping he'd say he should ask her out for coffee sometime. But I reminded myself that this was Wilson. He was nothing if not cautious. Maybe a card was a good starting place.

"Maybe so," I said. I frowned. "Actually, I just realized that Luna left her mom at home today. Sometimes it's better for Mona if she spends time at the library instead."

Wilson folded his arms together. "Why would she have left her at home? Especially on a bad day like this?"

"Well, I was over there very early this morning when everything happened. Mona was upset and wasn't ready to go anywhere at the time. But it's after lunch. Maybe she'd like to come over here now."

Wilson pulled up the library schedule on his computer. "But Luna has a storytime this afternoon."

I quickly added, "And I'm the only person covering the circulation desk. We have a couple of folks absent today or not scheduled."

Wilson looked uncomfortable, a slight ruddy color rising from his shirt collar. "I suppose I could offer to run over and pick Mona up."

I hid a smile at his discomfort. "It isn't a very long drive. I don't think it would be too awkward. And I'm sure she'd appreciate it."

He gave a brisk nod as if it were decided and before he could talk himself out of it, he picked up the phone. "The number?"

I gave it to him and he punched it in, clearing his throat. "Ms. Macon? This is . . . yes, hello. We were all very sorry to hear about your niece today. Such a terrible thing." He paused, listening. "I know you frequently like spending time at the library and aren't able to drive. Luna and Ann are tied up this afternoon, but I wondered if I might pick you up and bring you here, myself." He quickly added, "Only if that would provide a good distraction for you, of course."

Apparently, Mona accepted with alacrity because Wilson was now saying, "Good. Yes. I can be there in about fifteen minutes."

He put the receiver down, small beads of perspiration dotting his forehead. "Well. I suppose I should go ahead and head over there then."

Wilson had knocked me off-track by talking about the lunch with Grace and I hadn't even had a chance to speak with him about the volunteer luncheon arrangements. I hastily said, "It won't take you fifteen minutes to get there. Could I go over something with you really quick and see what you think?"

He suddenly turned his full attention back to me. "Ah, yes. Very good. I was going to ask you about that."

"I think I have a fairly good plan of how we should approach it."

Wilson frowned. "The Fitz Picks?"

I stared at him blankly. "Sorry?"

"You know—the pictures of Fitz and book displays. Fitz's faves. Something catchy like that. But it's not the kind of thing you need to get approval on, you know." Wilson was now stacking his papers and getting his car keys out of his desk drawer.

"We're speaking at cross-purposes, Wilson. I meant the volunteer appreciation luncheon."

He blinked at me. "Oh. That."

"Yes, that. I'd somehow gotten the impression the luncheon was something of a priority for the library."

He made a face. "Yes, I suppose so. Yes, of course it is. In my head, though, I wanted to move forward fairly quickly with the Fitz project. I think pictures of the cat with his favorite children's books, favorite new releases, favorite thrillers, etc. would make excellent posts on social media. They might even spark discussion and engagement. We could ask our audience who's read all the books in the photo. Or ask what books Fitz needs to read next."

I gave him a tight smile. "I'll get right on that."

"Good. And I do want to speak with you about the volunteer luncheon, naturally. Maybe sometime next week?" He was already walking toward the door, then frowned at seeing his reflection in his office window. He smoothed down his already-well-behaved hair.

"Perfect."

He said as he opened his office door. "At least you have a quiet afternoon to get cracking on it."

Chapter Sixteen

This, of course, was the kiss of death for the quiet afternoon. As soon as Wilson left to get Mona, the library became the busiest place in the town of Whitby. What's more, everyone needed to ask me a question.

When it was my break time, I hurried off to the lounge just as Luna was finishing up her own break and about to come out.

When Luna saw me, her eyes twinkled for the first real time that day. "Did you work some sort of magic, Ann?"

"Me?" I asked blankly.

"Yes, you! You're being far too modest. All I know is you had a meeting with Wilson and the next thing I knew, my mother was here at the library and Wilson himself was her driver."

Oh, of course. That's how busy the afternoon had been—it had eradicated any thought of Mona and Wilson. "To be honest, I went in his office to get the volunteer luncheon signed off on, but I did mention what happened to Roz. And I might have mentioned it would be good for your mom to come over to the library for a while today and get out of the house."

Luna rolled her eyes. "You never do take any credit. And then you somehow got him to pick her up. She was delighted.

You'd have thought Price Charming himself was at her door with a carriage."

"I simply explained to Wilson that you had storytime and that I was the sole librarian at the circulation desk." My eyes opened wide. "You don't mean they're actually hitting it off, do you? I had the feeling he was going to be all stiff and formal the whole way to the library."

Luna shrugged. "Maybe he started out that way, but when they came into the building, he was chuckling at something Mom said and she was beaming up at him. I mean, her eyes were still super-red from crying this morning, but I couldn't have dreamed up a better way of distracting her. Plus, with Wilson on his way over, she somehow got herself made-up and out of her pjs and robe and into a cute outfit in record time."

I smiled as I opened the fridge and pulled out the red grapes I'd brought in as a snack. "I'm so glad, Luna. I just hope he's nice to her. You know sometimes he's not even nice to *us*."

Luna waved her hand dismissively. "You're just saying that because sometimes he doesn't listen to us."

"Sometimes?" I asked.

"And he can be a little brusque."

I snorted again at 'a little.'

"But he has a heart of gold, you know. He'd do anything for you," said Luna.

I had to reluctantly agree with this. He was also an excellent manager, despite the not-listening thing. And he always had the library's best interests at heart.

"Besides," added Luna sweetly. "If he does anything to upset my mama, he's toast." She winked at me as she sailed out of the breakroom and back to her post in the children's section.

Things finally slowed down a bit and I was able to get started on Wilson's Fitz Picks or whatever he was going to call it.

Luna had pulled out some old picture book favorites (like *Mike Mulligan and His Steam Shovel*, *Corduroy*, and *The Story of Ferdinand*) and also came up with a stack of recent children's favorites (like *Brown Bear, Brown Bear, What Do You See?* and *Don't Let the Pigeon Drive the Bus!*) for me to use.

Then it was just up for me to see what sort of a mood Fitz was in. Not that he was ever in a *bad* mood, but sometimes it was easier to get a fetching photo of him than others, even though he was practically a pro at looking fetching. Sometimes, hard as it is to imagine, Fitz would rather just nap.

First, I had to locate Fitz, who'd disappeared while I'd been speaking with Luna in the breakroom earlier. He wasn't in any sunbeams. I strolled through the periodical section and looked in patron laps. No Fitz. Then I tiptoed through the quiet section trying not to distract the folks focusing on their studying, spreadsheets, taxes, or whatever else they might have been working on.

I frowned and walked over to the children's section again, although I hadn't noticed Fitz over there when I'd been over to see the books Luna had pulled out for me. She'd just finished giving book recommendations to a mom who wanted to encourage her son to read.

"Have you seen Fitz?" I asked.

She grinned and nodded. "Sure have. He's in the back corner with one of our young patrons."

I looked over at the back corner and sure enough, Fitz was fast asleep on the lap of an elementary-aged boy—a boy who was also asleep.

I winced. "I sort of hate to disturb them. Wilson wanted me to get moving on the Fitz's Picks thing, though. Has he been asleep long?"

"I don't think so. But he probably won't mind. Maybe he can even give you a hand with setting everything up. He looks to be about ten or eleven years old. You know you get the best photos when someone is playing with Fitz and you snap the photo."

This was true. Until I recruited people to help me snap playful pictures of Fitz, I had an excessive number of pictures of Fitz lying sleepily on his back.

I started walking toward the corner and called out softly, "Hey, there. May I take Fitz back?"

The boy woke up with a jolt, which wasn't what I'd intended. He hastily put the cat on the floor and took off.

I stopped, frowning and looked back toward Luna, who'd seen the whole thing.

"Maybe he realized there was something he needed to do," she said with a shrug. "Here, I can give you a hand with Fitz."

But as soon as she said it, a father came up with his son, needing help finding books to help with a report his child was doing for school. She gave me a helpless look and I collected Fitz to take the photos myself.

It didn't work out that way, though. Suddenly, the library became busy again. A patron asked for my help completing a job application on one of the shared computers. While I was helping her, another patron's shared computer froze and I had to help get it working again. Then a patron came in asking for a particular book: but couldn't remember the book's title or author, only that it had an orange cover. Fitz gave up on me and ended up taking a luxurious nap in a sunbeam in the periodical section.

After that—it was time for me to leave for the day since I was only on the schedule until four and it was already past that. Before I did, though, I wanted to ask Luna about what Linus had told me and I hadn't really had a chance earlier since Luna was focused on Wilson and her mother.

Luna was just re-shelving some picture books when I caught up with her. I mentioned what Linus had said about a long-ago tragedy and asked Luna if she knew anything about it.

She shook her head. "Not really—like I said, I was a good deal older, so I was already out of town. I'm sure my mom knows more about it, but I think she's playing cards with a couple of her friends near the periodicals."

I said quickly, "No worry, I'll check in with her later about it."

Luna glanced at the clock. "You should be getting out of here anyway or else you might find yourself stuck again."

A young mom came up to ask Luna something, so I headed back out of the children's section. I asked Fitz if he wanted to go home with me and he gave a chirping meow and padded toward the breakroom where I kept his carrier. He trotted happily into the cat carrier and I headed for the exit as quickly as possible, thinking patrons with problems might continue to ambush me on the way out.

Once I got back home, I fed Fitz, gave him some fresh water, and then rooted in my fridge to see what might be available for supper. I made a face at the unappealing offerings I saw. Maybe I'd gotten spoiled by going out with Grace. I didn't usually have a problem with my leftovers and they certainly needed to be eaten. But then, I didn't have that much of an appetite yet, either. The lunch, like most healthy food, had been very filling.

I walked to my bedroom and changed into athletic clothes. I hadn't gone jogging in years. It was one of those things I said I'd do at the start of the year but somehow never managed to follow through with. There was a moment of relief when I saw my athletic clothes still actually fit. I put on my running shoes, gave Fitz a quick rub, and headed back out to the car. I figured I'd run in the park instead of the neighborhood. Sometimes a change of scenery was a good thing.

The park was perfect, with wide sidewalks, views of the mountains, and a pond, complete with ducks, right in the middle with bridges to cross over the pond. It was busy there, but not too crazy. Several joggers, mothers with children who were feeding the ducks (the town had installed a bird feeding station to keep the public feedings safe for the ducks), and some kids playing in the playground there.

I realized I was going to have to stretch since I'd hadn't exercised for a while. Once I started stretching, I realized I was going to have to stretch quite a bit more. I hadn't realized how tight my muscles were until I started stretching. It couldn't all be from disuse—I was sure the stress from the past week was also taking its toll.

I was still working to get some more flexibility into my legs when I heard a voice behind me.

"Ann?"

I stopped stretching and turned to see Felicity there. She smiled at me. "So you *do* leave the library."

I chuckled. "Only occasionally and never successfully. I was planning on a run but then realized how tight all my muscles are. It looks like you're about to jog."

Felicity was decked out in what was likely very expensive athletic wear and not gear from Target, like I was. She smiled at me. "I am. I try to run every day."

"That's awesome," I said. "I need to do the same thing." I paused. "Actually, maybe a better goal would be once a week. Or once a month. If I say I'm going to run every day, it'll never happen."

"Well, with all the craziness lately, I'm *really* doing a lot of jogging. It's great stress-relief. Want to jog with me?"

"Right now?" I asked weakly.

Felicity chuckled. "Why not?"

I quickly said, "I don't think you know what you're getting into. I'll never be able to keep up your pace if you run every day."

"I'm not training for a marathon, just trying to move. Besides, it's supposed to be safer to jog with a buddy. Not that I'd ordinarily think of Whitby as a dangerous place, but . . ." She shrugged.

I reluctantly finally acquiesced and Felicity joined me in stretching. Then we took off at an easy pace. I could feel Felicity deliberately slowing down so we could run together.

Felicity glanced over at me. "Speaking of Whitby being unsafe, I heard about Roz. That's one reason I'm jogging right now . . . I'd already jogged this morning, but the news really stressed me out."

I said slightly breathlessly, "Yes, it was a real shock. I didn't know Roz as well as the rest of you did of course, but I really liked her. And I felt terrible for Luna."

Felicity added, "And Kelly. Whenever I think of Kelly, I think of Roz. They're like peanut butter and jelly." She sighed. "Anyway, I don't know what to make of it. Have you heard any details about what happened from Luna? I tried to reach Kelly today, but her phone went right to voice mail."

I slowed my pace just a little so I would be able to jog and talk at the same time. "I don't know much. I know it looks like someone waited for Roz to leave for her shift and then pushed her down the stairs."

"It wasn't an accident then?" asked Felicity. Her eyes narrowed. "Part of me was hoping poor Roz was in a hurry, took a wrong step and landed in a bad way on the staircase."

I shook my head. "It doesn't appear so."

"And it wasn't a mugging gone wrong? A robbery?"

I shook my head again. "Nothing was stolen."

Felicity said roughly, "What a mess. This whole thing is like a nightmare that won't stop. First the odd weekend party ending with Scott's death. Now Roz? I mean, what's going on?"

I didn't respond, partly because I hoped Felicity would go on talking and partly because I was more out of breath than I should be.

Felicity continued, "I'm sure everybody is thinking the same thing, but who would kill Roz? She was always a peacemaker. Always a supportive friend. I just can't believe someone I know would do something like this."

"What do you think might have happened?" I asked, gasping a little.

Felicity sighed. "I just don't know." She paused for a few moments, which I was grateful for as I tried to regulate my breathing. "The only thing I can think of is that Roz knew something about what happened to Scott. The morning we found Scott in the pool, I was talking with Roz and felt like she wasn't being completely forthcoming. When I pushed her on it, she just shook her head and said she wasn't going to ruin somebody's life over something she wasn't sure even happened. Now she's dead."

"You think she might have been covering up for somebody," I said.

Felicity shrugged. "I don't know what else to think. But I know Roz said she had a lot to drink that night and she was worried her memory wasn't all that reliable. Or that maybe she got the events out of order."

I said, "I'm sure everybody feels that way. There was a lot of alcohol and lots of sun that day."

"Yeah."

I said carefully, "I think both the drinks and the sun made everybody act out more than they usually would. Kyle seemed upset at Scott's flirtatious behavior over the weekend, too."

Felicity snorted. "Scott was just trying to get under Kelly's skin."

"You weren't upset about Scott's advances? I think I might have been." I tried to keep my voice light.

"Oh no. No, I knew exactly what Scott was doing and I gave him a piece of my mind about it. He backed off after that."

I said slowly, "Do you think Scott was also trying to get a rise out of Kyle?"

Felicity flushed and I didn't think it was from the jogging. "What do you mean?"

"It's just that Kyle seemed like he might be interested in you, that's all."

Felicity was quiet for a couple of moments. "I don't know. Although I find that hard to believe. Kyle and I have known each other for so long that we're almost like brother and sister."

It hadn't looked that way to me, but I kept quiet. I wasn't even entirely sure I could summon enough breath to speak.

Felicity finally added, "Actually, I wouldn't mind going out with Kyle, although it would be a little weird at first. Like I said, we've known each other since we were kids. But I can't do it with a murder investigation hanging over us. I want Scott's and Roz's deaths to be cleared up and then maybe we can see where we stand."

I glanced over at her. "I have the feeling he's going to try and attend that next book club meeting."

Felicity said, "I'll be sure to be prepared to tell him the same thing I told you—we need to hold off until this investigation is finished."

"Speaking of finished," I said in a gasping voice. "I think I'm done for today. I'm going to drop off and let you get a real run in."

Felicity grinned at me. "Want to meet up with me tomorrow? Same time, same place?"

I shook my head as I realized with relief that I was scheduled late at the library. "Think I'm working then."

"Too bad. See you at the library." And Felicity, increasing her pace, jogged away.

I knew I needed to cool down and not just abruptly sit on a bench, which was what I really wanted to do. So I slowed my pace to a slow walk in an attempt to get my heart rate down. I spotted a large dog and an elderly man heading in my direction, then took a second look as I realized it was Linus. Smiling, I headed toward him.

He stopped and, amazingly, so did the dog. Linus looked pleased.

"Wow, she's really responsive to you," I said. "And well-behaved. I'd have thought she'd try jumping on me or get excited and start pulling on the leash. Her name is Ivy, isn't it?"

Linus looked proud as he looked down at the dog. "Ivy, yes. She's been really good. Maybe she knows I'm older and she's being careful not to run."

"Or maybe you two already have a close connection. It sure seems that way." And it did. Ivy was looking up at Linus as if she were waiting on a cue from him.

Then he gave her one. "Sit," he said quietly and Ivy plopped right down. He gave her a treat and the dog grinned up at him.

I blinked at the dog in surprise. "Wow. So . . . do you think she learned that from a previous owner?"

He smiled at Ivy. "I'd have thought that too, except she didn't know the command at all about two hours ago. We've been working on it. She seems really bright."

Usually two hours ago would have been a time when Linus would still have been ensconced in the library—at that point reading fiction. I thought back over the day and realized I hadn't noticed him in there at all.

He must have somehow read my mind because he said shyly, "It felt a little odd not being in the library today."

I chuckled. "Believe me, I know the feeling. I'm so rarely *not* at the library that when I have a day off, I keep thinking the whole day that I've forgotten something. But I'm being paid to be there. It's probably *good* for you to do shake things up every now and then."

Linus nodded. "It was just such a beautiful day. Then the vet called me this morning and said Ivy was ready to go home with me. I went to the store to buy her a pet bed and toys and a few other things and then picked her up."

"I bet she was glad to see you," I said.

His eyes twinkled. "Her whole body wagged. But she didn't jump on me. She's very polite."

Ivy flopped on her back for a tummy rub and Linus and I complied. "This is what I should have done," I said with a chuckle. "Walked. You have the right idea, Linus."

"Did you run?" he asked in the kind of tone that indicated running was something far out of his sphere of experience.

I nodded. "I did. I've only just gotten my breath back, too. In future, I'll have to remind myself there's nothing wrong with a brisk walk instead." I always tried to be cognizant of the amount of time Linus felt comfortable in conversation so I gave Ivy a final pat and said, "I'll leave you two to it. Time for me to head back home. Fitz is probably ready for a little supper."

Linus smiled at me and said, "If you ran, you're probably ready for a little supper, too."

As I drove home, I realized it was true. Not only was I starving, though, I knew from earlier there was nothing very appetizing in my house. I had things to snack on like carrot sticks and stuff for making sandwiches, but I knew I'd have a sandwich and carrot sticks for lunch tomorrow at the library and I didn't much want them two meals in a row. I remembered I didn't even have eggs in the house and at that point decided to make a run to the store.

One thing about living in a small town—there wasn't a lot of choice when it came to grocery stores. In fact, there was only one store that was convenient to most of the town. Consequently, there also wasn't a lot of choice when it came to food items. Most of the time I didn't really need a bunch of options, but I would have killed that night for a full-service deli section with some already-prepared food ready to pop into the oven to heat up. There were a few offerings in the small deli section and I stood there for a few minutes deliberating the pros and cons of spaghetti (which didn't seem to have much sauce) and chicken and broccoli (which likewise didn't appear to have sauce. Or, perhaps, even seasoning).

A voice came from behind me and I startled a little. "Go with the spaghetti. Trust me."

Chapter Seventeen

I turned around to see Kyle standing there with an apologetic grin. "Sorry for making you jump. It's just that I happen to have experience with both of those meals and the spaghetti is far superior in every way. Even better if you have extra red sauce and grated parmesan cheese at home."

"Thanks. Sounds like the best choice tonight, anyhow. I'm too beat to try to think of something to put together myself. And you didn't really scare me—I've just been jumpy lately."

Kyle's expression darkened. "I'd imagine so. I have been, too." He paused and then said, "I guess you've heard about Roz. I mean, working with Luna and everything. Is Luna doing okay? And her mom?"

I nodded. "I think they're okay. Luna wanted to come right back into work, though, to stay busy and not have as much time to think."

"I bet she did. I've been trying to stay busy the last few days, myself. I helped out Scott's mother and brother in Scott's house today." His expression darkened. "It was tough on them."

"I can imagine," I said softly.

He added slowly, "They seemed to be getting a different picture of Scott the longer we cleared his things out. Finally, they took a break and I kept going for another hour or so."

"A different picture of him? Like how?"

He quickly said, "Oh, I don't know. Just that Scott has always created this image of himself as being so successful. And they were realizing what bad shape his finances were in. Stuff like that." He changed the subject. "I keep running everything through my head, trying to figure out what must have happened. But I don't ever seem to get anywhere with it because I *know* everyone and I hit a wall every time. I mean, Kelly was mad at Scott. Really mad. But would she have killed him? And then murdered her best friend to cover everything up?"

I didn't say anything and Kyle continued, "I can't see it. I can *kind* of see her killing Scott in the heat of the moment. But from what I heard, the attack on Roz was planned out."

I nodded. And I glanced around to make sure no one could overhear Kyle, but the deli section was deserted and the worker wasn't even behind the counter.

Kyle said, "And Grace. Why would Grace have killed Scott? For ruining her party weekend?" He shook his head. "It just doesn't add up." He looked at me. "You didn't even know any of the people involved, so you couldn't have done it unless you're some sort of psychopath or something."

I gave a startled laugh that likely did sound like something a psychopath would utter.

He absently reached for a spaghetti dinner for himself as he continued his analysis. "Luna had no connection with Scott and she loved Roz. No reason for her to be responsible."

"And Felicity?" I asked.

Kyle snorted as if the possibility was so outrageous it never even occurred to him. "There's no way Felicity would ever be involved in something like this. She's very civic-minded and contributes to society. Why on earth would she ever kill Scott Haynsworth?"

I shrugged and said in a light tone, "If we're listing possibilities, no matter how farfetched, then surely Scott's unwelcome attention could be considered a motive."

Kyle scowled. "No, because she's fully capable of handling Scott's boorish behavior herself. And she did—by avoiding him and then turning in early." The mention of Scott's actions seemed to turn his mood much darker.

"And you?" I asked, still in that light tone.

"Me?" Kyle stared blankly at me.

"Well, we considered me as a possible suspect. What about you? What motives would you have had?"

Kyle shrugged as if this line of questioning was of no consequence. "I wouldn't have. I've known Scott my entire life. I was devastated when I found out he was dead. Losing someone you've known since childhood is a terrible blow."

I said slowly, "Someone mentioned you might carry some resentment over a long-ago business deal that went badly."

Kyle snapped, "Someone should keep their mouth shut, especially since they don't have the facts straight." He blew out a sigh. "Sorry. Small towns. I'll never get used to everyone knowing everything."

"What did they get wrong?" I asked.

He shrugged. "The business deal wasn't *bad*. Scott merely bought me out. Could it have been a better deal? Sure. In hindsight, the business ended up doing extremely well and I should have counteroffered for more money. But think about it; the business was in its infancy. How would we have known how successful it would end up? It might have done exactly the opposite and completely failed."

"Was the decision to leave the business your idea or Scott's?" I asked curiously.

Kyle rubbed his face. "It was long enough ago that I honestly don't remember how it came about. But I know I wasn't cut out for the day-to-day operation of building and running a business." He gave me a rueful smile. "Believe it or not, Scott was the charming one. He was the front-man for us. Scott spoke with investors and was good at putting together marketing strategies and just making the whole thing work. He was a numbers guy and I was an idea guy. So, yeah, maybe I wasn't keen on running a business. Maybe Scott and I came to that same conclusion simultaneously. I don't know."

I asked, "Did you continue dreaming up business ideas? I'd think that would take a lot of ingenuity."

Kyle gave a short laugh. "As a matter of fact, I haven't. Maybe I was a one-trick pony and that was my only trick. The start-up took a good deal of my time to develop. I probably should have spent more of that time trying to figure out what I wanted to do with my life *after* the start-up. When Scott bought me out, I was suddenly left without anything. I felt like I was scrambling after that. And it probably didn't help that Scott's business was suddenly taking off." He added quickly, "I was still proud that it was doing so well. I knew I had a real hand in its success. But I was . . . lost."

"What did you do after that?" I asked.

He sighed. "Well, I put off deciding what to do. Although I actually had a fairly good reason for that—my mother was ailing and having a hard time kicking it. I helped her out and got sucked into life there. Different doctor appointments a few days a week, cleaning, helping her with her yard work. In hindsight, it was good for me because I had a place to live and a routine of sorts while I figured out what to do next. But I had one job opportunity I had to turn down because it was in another state. The problem is, my timing has always been lousy."

"What happened then?" I asked.

"I floundered for a while. Scott was aware of it, too. He called me once and offered to take me on at the business."

I raised my eyebrows. "But you said you weren't interested in running a company."

"I wasn't. But Scott wasn't offering to take me on as a partner—only as an employee."

I'd detected a note of bitterness in Kyle's voice. "That must have stung."

He nodded. "It did. But it was still pretty nice of the guy. He offered to let me work remotely so I could stay at home with my mom. But I ended up turning it down."

"You obviously found a direction, though," I said, trying to encourage him.

He gave me a wry smile. "Did I somehow give that impression? I'm not sure how. No, I'm afraid I'm currently unemployed. I've floated from job to job like a dandelion seed. And that hasn't helped my personal life, either. Most of my adult life I've been living with my mom and trying to find a solid job. It's not easy to find dates that way."

I said, "Felicity and you seem to have a nice connection." I paused as he flushed. "I'm sorry, I hope you don't think I'm being nosy."

He shook his head, still a little flustered. "No, of course not. After all, I approached you to find out what book club Felicity was talking about. Naturally you'd be curious about that."

"You've known each other for a long time," I said.

"We have. Maybe *too* long. It could be one of those things where Felicity sees me as more of a brother because we've always hung out together."

Better a brother than a murder suspect. Felicity was one of those people who held things close to her chest. It was tough to get a good read on whether she was interested in Kyle romantically or not.

Kyle rubbed his forehead as if it was starting to hurt. "Another problem is that I have another reason for wanting to talk to Felicity. She has a lot of business contacts in neighboring towns and I wondered if she'd help me network to find another job. Not at *her* job, of course. That would be too weird, especially if I want to have any kind of relationship with her."

I said gently, "Have you thought about just calling her?"

Kyle frowned. "What do you mean?"

"I mean, it seems to me like you're knocking yourself out trying to casually run into her. You're planning on showing up to her book club."

Kyle said, "I like to read, though."

"And you've used every opportunity to try and sit near her . . . at least, when I've been around. But there's a lot going on with all of us right now. I think being direct is probably the best approach when life gets crazy."

"You really think so?" Kyle's face was worried. "I don't know. I haven't ever really just called her up like that." He added thoughtfully, "Although, in the past, I thought that being direct was the way to go. You probably won't believe this, but for a while, every time he and I would go out to supper or catch a movie or something, he'd invited Roz to go along with us."

"Really?" I couldn't see Roz and Scott together. Especially after Roz had yelled at him at the party.

"Oh, not for Scott. I think he was planning on Roz and me hitting it off romantically. He'd do things like that sometimes. He liked the idea of being a matchmaker, but he never threw the right people together. And now they're both gone." He cleared his throat and gave me an apologetic smile. "I've kept you here way too long when you're just trying to grab some supper and get back home. I'll see you soon. At the library, I'm sure." He gave me a crooked grin and disappeared into the cereal aisle.

I walked through the checkout line with my spaghetti and a side of mashed potatoes. I had the feeling I might be totally undoing the effects of my jogging, but I was definitely in the mood for carbs.

Fitz greeted me joyfully, as always. He was as good as a dog for making a person feel good. When he looked at you it was as if he was saying: *You! I've been waiting to see you all day long. Hi, friend.* I heated up my supper and Fitz immediately jumped up into the kitchen chair that was the next one over and seemed to smile at me as I ate. He was perfectly polite, though, and didn't hop into my lap until I was completely finished eating and once I'd invited him to.

I was scratching Fitz under his chin and listening to his rumbling purr when my phone rang. I looked at it apprehensively. The phone calls I'd gotten lately hadn't been the best. I reluctantly leaned forward and grabbed it from the far side of the table. My heart gave an extra couple of beats when I saw it was Grayson calling and I worked hard to keep my voice steady as I answered.

"Hi there," he said easily. "Hope I'm not interrupting anything."

I felt like I should mention I was actually doing something fascinating and exciting. But considering I'd just finished up a ready-to-eat meal from the grocery deli and my entertainment consisted of loving on Fitz, I decided not to. "Not a bit," I said, trying to keep my tone as light as his. "Just hanging out with Fitz."

"That's good. Listen, just wanted to let you know that I've had great response to your library column. You did an awesome job with that."

"Really?" my voice sounded as doubtful as I felt. I didn't doubt that the column was decent—I figured anyone who was interested in either reading or the library would find it at least helpful. But I was certainly surprised that there would actually be feedback one way or another to the newspaper office.

"Sure. Wow, you sound surprised," he said with a chuckle.

"It's just that I didn't think anyone would give you feedback," I said.

"Are you kidding? In Whitby? The newspaper gets feedback on every tiny thing. It appears there are plenty of people here who don't have a lot to do. I made the mistake of discontinuing what apparently was a beloved comic strip and replacing it with one of the latest, coolest strips out there."

I smiled. "I'm guessing that strategy didn't work out well."

"It was catastrophic! At one point I wondered if an angry mob might gather outside the newspaper office and start throwing stones at me when I arrived for work. Believe me, I very quickly brought the favorite old strip back. I wouldn't think about making any changes to the newspaper without lots of deliberation."

I said teasingly, "Well, that makes me feel good, knowing the new column could have ended up instigating riots."

"Yes, you should feel good about yourself. I got two phone calls right away on it and then a few emails. Everyone was in favor of the column and most of them were also staunch Ann Beckett fans, too. I didn't realize I'd solicited a local celebrity for the column." His voice was teasing too and I felt warmth course through me in response.

I chided myself. Where did I think this was going, anyway? He wasn't interested in me the same way or we'd already be an item.

He continued, "Anyway, I thought I might start tackling the trail reviews and see what the response is to those. I know you're busy, but I wondered if you have any breaks in your schedule and can point out some good trails to me. Or, even better, maybe go on one or two of them."

I'd already been mulling this over since the first time he spoke with me about it. Honestly, what did I have to lose? I've been trying to exercise more and get out more and clearly jogging wasn't my favorite thing. Maybe my feelings for Grayson were more of a crush, anyway, and the more time I spent with him, the more disillusioned I'd become. Maybe.

"Sure," I said finally. "I think I'm off in a few days. If the weather's good, let's do it. I can give you a couple of different options for trails and see what you think: difficulty level, view, etc. I'll email you tomorrow."

"Great!" Grayson's voice was pleased. "And I'll leave you alone for the night. Give Fitz a rub for me."

Once I hung up, I swore Fitz was looking at me with a sympathetic expression on his face. I was frequently guilty of anthropomorphizing Fitz and thinking of him as a rather small and hairy human. But then he bumped his head lovingly against my face as if to comfort me. He was more cued in to emotions than any other cat I'd ever seen.

I rubbed him under his chin in return and sighed. "Thanks, Fitz. I think it will work out all right."

I thought Fitz's eyes held just the slightest amount of doubt in them.

Unfortunately, between thinking and talking about Roz all day and the late conversation with Grayson, sleep proved frustratingly elusive that night. I gave up even trying to sleep around 3:30. Fitz opened a surprised eye when I got out of the bed, but he stayed curled up in a ball at the foot of my bed as if to demonstrate proper sleeping methods.

Sometimes, when I couldn't sleep and my mind was whirling, it was better to just do a brain dump of all the things I needed to do or the thoughts I was having. If it was a task that needed to be done, I stuck it on my calendar. If it was just a nagging thought, sometimes it stopped pestering me if it was down on paper. Sitting in my robe and fuzzy socks, I scribbled in a composition notebook until I couldn't think of anything else on my mind. I wrote ideas for walking trails with Grayson and tips for keeping it all on a professional level (i.e., no doe eyes from me when I looked at Grayson). I wrote about the Fitz's Picks pictures and ideas for what titles to include.

Then I moved on to Scott's and Roz's deaths. I made little notes about Kyle's business dealings with Scott and his interest in Felicity. I wrote about Scott needing a tax attorney. I jotted down how Felicity had been trying to ignore Scott. I made a note about Roz's room location overlooking the pool, her comments to Kelly, and her murder. I considered Kelly and Scott's troubled relationship. Then I put down Grace's collection of guests and the words she'd exchanged with Scott when I'd woken up from my nap on the boat.

I read everything I'd written, and then picked up my laptop. I didn't know as much about Felicity and Grace as I felt I did about the other guests at the party. I started searching for their names online: social media, press releases, newspaper articles.

Felicity came up a few times and it all seemed to be work-related. She headed a volunteer group that tutored in local elementary schools, she received some sort of banking award for meeting a particular goal, she joined an industry-related organization. She wore a tight smile in each photo I saw of her and her eyes looked deeply reproachful as if she was unhappy with the photographer about taking her picture.

Grace was much the same way, except that she seemed to *enjoy* having her photo taken and appeared to be genuinely enjoying herself in the pictures I saw. There was an obituary for her husband, who'd been a bit older than Grace. Actually, he'd been quite a bit older. They'd been very active together in their community and were photographed at a lot of banquets and charitable events. Grace wore expensive-looking gowns, her husband wore tuxedos, and they were with people who were equally well-attired in formal settings.

I started delving into Grace's deceased husband's information, which took time since most of the stories about him related to philanthropy. I raised my eyebrows when I read that he was a major shareholder and board member in a pharmaceutical company. The main product for the company was an opioid that had been on the news quite a bit. I frowned. The opioid had been blamed for a lot of misery around the country in general. Maybe that explained why her husband had been such a philanthropist; he felt guilty.

The problem was that there wasn't anything for either Felicity or Grace that went back any farther than five years or so. I decided when I got back to work that I might look in the archives at the paper and see if there was anything from when they attended college. Or, perhaps, even earlier. The paper had digitized some back issues, but it seemed it was a large, ongoing project that was only addressed when someone on staff had time .. . or maybe an intern. I decided to ask Grayson about it the next time I spoke to him. Fortunately, the library had a collection of all the newspaper archives, although some of them were still on microfiche. I'd have to see how busy we were at work.

I glanced at the clock and saw with surprise that I'd managed to burn up a couple of hours. I fed Fitz, who was now sleepily waking up, and did some stretching since I'd been hunched over my computer. I ate my breakfast, packed my lunch for the day, and tried to use makeup to address the fact that my eyes had bags under them from the sleepless night.

It still wasn't quite time to head off to work, so I read *And Then There Were None* for a while, finishing it up in the process. It gave me the willies even more than usual since Roz's murder. It also made me think. In Agatha Christie's story, the consecutive murders were connected to sins in each person's past. It made me even more determined to poke around in the archives. And, maybe, speak with Luna. After all, she remembered everyone from when they were in school. Maybe she could shed some light on them.

Chapter Eighteen

Fitz and I arrived at the library thirty minutes before it opened. I loved the library when it was quiet like this. It almost made it feel like it was something that belonged totally to me. Fitz, although incredibly social for a cat, also liked the chance to sprawl out in the middle of the library floor for a nap—something he was cautious about doing when the library was full.

Wilson came in fifteen minutes later, looking pleased to see me there. "Excellent! You're getting an early start on the day, aren't you?"

"I figured I might as well, since I was up early this morning," I said lightly. My voice, I realized, didn't sound exactly like myself, though. It was a scratchy, throaty, didn't-get-enough-sleep voice.

Wilson frowned and said, "Yes, seems you did. Hopefully not *too* early. I believe you're closing up this evening, aren't you?"

That was actually a wrinkle I'd forgotten about. I repressed a sigh. It was going to be a long day on *both* ends, it seemed. I nodded.

"Well, what have you gotten started on this morning?" asked Wilson briskly. "Might as well have a look before I head into the office and all the paperwork devours me."

I hadn't really made my notes about Fitz's Picks for public viewing and they were hastily scribbled out. I flipped to the page in my notebook and showed Wilson my very sketchy sketches and the titles I'd come up with as the cat's favorites in different categories.

Wilson nodded, looking pleased again. "That's going to work very well, I think. Yes, very well." He paused. "On other matters, I was wondering if you'd heard anything from Grace?"

I chuckled. "Are you proposing I start a daily lunch club with her? No, I'm afraid I haven't."

Wilson said, "No, no, nothing like that. I was simply curious if she thought renaming the community room was a good idea."

"I haven't even broached it with her yet. We've been talking about other things." I hesitated, thinking about her husband and the opioid income. "Just a thought and you're welcome to ignore it if you like. But usually the consensus is that it's safer to name a building or a room after someone long-dead and not someone who's still living."

Wilson frowned at this. "I can't imagine us going wrong with naming a room after Grace Armstrong. It's hardly likely there's going to be a scandal of some sort."

"I know. I'm not saying there is, is just that perhaps we should proceed with caution. Maybe the board needs to vote on it, for one."

"The board?" Wilson stared at me as if I were from outer space. Considering how early I'd arisen, perhaps I was starting to look a bit alien. "The board doesn't have to be involved in trivial decisions like this. It's a waste of their time." His eyes narrowed. "Is there something you know about Grace that I don't?"

The last thing I wanted to do was gossip, especially during my early-morning quiet time at the library before things started getting busy. But now Wilson was looking at me as if he expected a far-worse story, so I supposed I needed to spill what little I knew. "It's really probably nothing. It's just that Grace's money, from what I understand, came to her from her husband's estate when he passed away."

Wilson said irritably, "And there's nothing wrong with that. It's her money now, isn't it?"

"Of course it is. All I'm saying is I spent a bit of time doing some research. You know how research librarians are," I said, trying to keep my voice light.

Wilson's eyes narrowed even further so they were slits behind his glasses.

I took a deep breath. "Anyway, her husband was on the board and owned a lot of stock in a pharmaceutical company. The company had a few smaller products that didn't bring in much income. Their star product and the bulk of the business's income came from an opioid drug. The company has had lots of bad press and so have the board members and others associated with the business." Wilson's face was unreadable and I continued, "It was all online. I read a good number of articles on it all."

Wilson now looked as if he devoutly wished I weren't such a nosy person. Or such an avid researcher. "And you're sure about this?"

"Very sure. I can send you links, if you'd like to read the stories."

He shook his head and put up a hand as if warding off unhappy stories. "No. No, I don't think I want to." He paused for several moments and then said slowly, "I suppose one could say the money is tainted. Yes, I don't think it would be too dramatic to say it's tainted with human unhappiness and desperation."

This was quite a poetic turn of phrase for Wilson.

He paused again and then said, "Yes. Yes, I think you may be right. I should present this to the board. Perhaps they'll think it's more appropriate to return the funds, under these circumstances, and not risk putting the library in a bad light. Or," he added hopefully, "maybe they'll think it's an opportunity for the money to be used for public good since it was used to harm the public previously. At any rate, I shouldn't make the decision on my own. Good point, Ann."

He started moving briskly away to his office and then stopped and turned around. "When I present this issue to the board, I would like to come fully-apprised. On second thoughts, could you send me all the links and information you have?"

I pulled out a sheet of paper from my purse and handed it wordlessly to him.

He nodding, glancing over it as if not at all surprised that such a document existed. "And could you continue more delving into Grace's background? It appears we have abundant information on her husband, but not so much on Grace herself. Particularly if we're to name a room in the library after her."

I said, "Actually, that was something I was going to tackle today if it's not too busy here."

Wilson shook his head. "We have tons of staff and volunteers here today. I looked at the schedule last night. The library can spare you, believe me."

"It's going to mean spending a good deal of time in the archive room with old newspapers. The local paper didn't start putting their articles online until about ten years ago."

Wilson shook his head again, this time with some irritation. I wasn't sure if it was irritation at me for continuing to press the point, or irritation with the newspaper for not loading their archives online. "Whatever it takes."

"Actually, Luna might be able to provide some additional information, as well. And maybe her mother. They knew Grace from when she was growing up here."

Wilson said, "Please call Luna and ask her to bring her mother to the library with her today." He flushed slightly and then resumed his brisk path to his office where he firmly closed the door behind him.

Luna was more than happy to bring her mother to the library, although it meant Mona had to quickly dress since Luna had been about to leave the house to head to work. I smiled to see Mona arriving at the library with a large makeup bag and quickly disappearing into the restroom to finish getting ready. Luna appeared to be carrying a covered dish of some sort.

"Breakfast casserole for the breakroom," she said wryly.

I blinked at it. "How on earth did Mona know she would be here today?"

"Oh, she intended on bringing it for us tomorrow, but she cooked it last night in preparation. Her whole strategy for wooing Wilson is via food," said Luna.

"I think she may be winning the battle. Wilson seems to be blushing quite a bit."

"That's good to hear," grinned Luna. "I'd hate to think all this cooking could be for nothing. Nothing, aside from a bunch of extra calories I don't really need."

I followed Luna into the breakroom as she put the labeled casserole in the fridge. "By the way, our day is taking something of a detour. Courtesy of Wilson."

"Is it?" asked Luna, looking surprised. "Wilson isn't so fond of detours."

"He wants us to help him find out more information on Grace." I quickly gave her the low-down on the origins of Grace's wealth.

Luna gave a low whistle. "So now he wants you to dig up as much dirt as possible on her. I see how it is."

I winced. Luna always had a way of getting to the heart of the matter. "I don't know if I'd really look at it that way. He said he wanted to go to the board with as much information as possible."

Luna said glumly, "There go our lovely lunches. I knew it was too good to last."

"And now we're going to spend our day shut up in the dusty archives room. Wilson said he had lots of help today. Apparently, he overscheduled volunteers and staff, so we're covered."

Luna raised her eyebrows. "Even in the children's area? Wow, okay. Well, let's see what we can uncover." She glanced over at Wilson's closed door and rolled her eyes. "The least he could do is come out of his office. My mom is putting time into getting her makeup just right for him."

"He'll definitely want that breakfast casserole. Your mom should let him know it's in there."

Luna shook her head. "She'd never be so forward as to knock on his closed office door. I guess I could do it, though, before we get started."

While Luna was giving Wilson a heads-up about the breakfast food, I eyed the newspaper archive. Our older newspapers were all on microfiche, but the old papers from the early 2000s hadn't been transferred because microfiche was falling out of fa-vor at that point as everyone was hopping online. Everyone, it seems, but the Whitby newspaper.

Luna came back as I started pulling out papers from around the time the whole group would have been in high school.

"Any ideas about where I should start?" I asked.

Luna blew out a breath as her gaze combed the wall of pa-pers. "I really don't know what Wilson is looking for. Couldn't we just do a background check on her with Burton?"

I gave her a doubtful look. "Somehow I don't see Burton happily doing a background check without good reason. I think Wilson is trying to make sure there's nothing on Grace that pre-dates the online stuff we've already found. But I feel if there was something on her, you'd probably know about it, right? Small town. I should probably know about it too, but I wasn't paying that much attention to what older kids were doing when I was a kid."

Luna said, "The problem is that when Roz and her friends were in high school, I'd already left Whitby and was making a living in New York. I *kind* of kept up, but not really. You know what college is like." She frowned. "Like I mentioned, I know there was a tragedy with the group, but I don't have any real de-tails."

I said, "That's the one Linus mentioned to me."

She nodded. "I asked my mom about it briefly last night. One of their friends died. They were all out on the lake together. I think they'd skipped school or something. It was one of those stories that the local moms would tell their kids to keep them in line. Anyway, they skipped school and went out to the lake for the day and one of their friends drowned, I think. She wasn't even very far from the shoreline so it was probably a cramp."

I stared at her. "Luna, that's awful! That must have really scarred all of them."

Luna said, "Of course it did. I think Roz still had nightmares sometimes about it."

"And they saw her drown? Or did she sort of slip off to swim and went missing?"

Luna said, "I'm not really sure. I don't think all of them were around when it happened. Mom was fuzzy on the details and I'm fuzzy on repeating them." She frowned. "Actually, I think maybe Felicity and Scott were around and the others were taking a walk or something. From what I remember, they tried to help the girl . . . it was a girl . . . but by the time they reached her, it was too late. But we're talking about something that happened decades ago, Ann. It's not like it was a recent tragedy or anything."

"Well, the paper would definitely have reported a story like that. It's rare that something like that happens here. Most of the articles in the Whitby paper have to do with who's become an Eagle Scout or whose vegetable garden has a prize-winning tomato." I started rooting around in the papers.

Luna said, "You won't get too far with that. The paper wouldn't have reported the names because they were minors at the time. They have a policy against doing that."

I stared at the stack of papers and said, "It doesn't really sound like the type of story Wilson is looking for, anyway. He's trying to find out if there were any scandals that would make the library embarrassed by naming a room after Grace. A tragedy when she was a teenager doesn't fit the bill. And it sounds like she wasn't even around at the time it happened, even if she was part of the group."

Wilson opened the door to the archive room then. He had a slightly panicked expression on his face, which eased slightly as soon as he spotted us. "There you are."

I bit my tongue to keep from replying that we were exactly where he'd asked us to be. And apparently Luna wasn't feeling in a sassy mood either, because she also didn't say anything.

"Plans have changed," said Wilson briskly. "You're needed out front."

"What happened?" I asked. How did we go from over-staffed to understaffed in a matter of minutes?

Wilson sighed. "The schedule was incorrect. I must have been interrupted in the middle of creating it. We're not over-staffed at all; in fact, we could use a few extra people. Did you find anything out?"

Luna said, "We didn't have time to dig into the archives, but I remembered a tragedy that happened when Grace was a teenager."

"Did she cause the tragedy?" asked Wilson intently.

Luna shook her head.

"Did she *indirectly* cause the tragedy?" he asked.

Luna shook her head.

"Then it's nothing of concern. Case closed. And I'll present the information I do have to the board at our next meeting." Wilson trotted away.

Luna left to take on the children's section. I hesitated. There was something about this death that didn't sit right with me.

I took my phone out of my pocket and dialed Burton, hoping I wasn't completely sending him on a tangent and wasting his time.

"Hey there," he said, sounding very much as if he was in the middle of something. "What's up?"

"Maybe nothing," I said. "But I wanted to loop you in on a couple of things, in case you didn't know." I quickly told him first about Grace's husband's wealth.

Burton said, "I appreciate it, but we've actually already found that information out. It doesn't seem to tie into the case, though. If one of the others in the group had lost someone close to them from opioid addiction, we'd definitely have a motive. Right now, it just explains how Grace ended up with so much money."

I took a deep breath. "Got it. There's something else, too. I don't want to send you on a wild goose chase, though."

Burton chuckled. "Oh, I love me a wild goose chase. Go ahead and lay it on me. You never know if it might end up being something important. Besides, you're not the kind of person who comes up with totally innocuous stuff. You're a research librarian, after all."

"At any rate, I'm not sure if it means anything. So, when all of the group was in high school together, they cut school one day and took off for the lake." I glanced at the door, expecting Wilson to come barreling through it at any moment to drag me off to the circulation desk.

There was a pause on the other end. "Okay, I take it all back. This is totally innocuous stuff."

I laughed. "Sorry, there's more. I was just distracted for a second, sorry. While they were there, a member of their party drowned."

Now I had Burton's attention again. "Was it a suspicious death?"

"Well, I was going to try to find out information from our newspaper archives, but Luna pointed out that the newspaper's policy is to redact names if the people involved are under the age of eighteen, which apparently they all were at the time. I wondered if there was more to the story and if you could possibly check back in the police department records to see what you could find out."

Burton said, "Sure. I'm on it. You just never know."

I said, "I did want to follow-up on one thing with you, if you're able to tell me. Did you ask Grace if Scott was blackmailing her?"

"I did. I didn't mention your name, so no worries about that. She said Scott was being pushy about a loan. He said Grace owed him for introducing her to her late-husband."

It sure hadn't sounded that way to me, but I didn't have any proof otherwise.

There was a voice in the background and then he said, "Got to run. Thanks for the call." And he hung up.

Chapter Nineteen

Wilson was right about needing a few extra people. I didn't end up taking my breaks and my lunch "hour" was spent in the lounge eating as fast as I could shove the food down my throat before hurrying back out to the front desk.

Things started easing a little at six, but I still had three hours left to go since I was locking up. The lack of sleep from the night before was definitely catching up with me and I couldn't stop yawning. Considering the concerned looks the patrons were giving me, I had the feeling I had that lovely hollow-eyed look I got when I was totally exhausted. In some ways, the busyness of the day had helped me get through, but now things were slowing down, tiredness was hitting me like a sledgehammer.

Luna and her mom came by the desk to say goodbye as they were on their way out the door. Her mother was beaming because Wilson had complimented her on the breakfast casserole: a fact she confided to me with a happy smile.

I said ruefully, "I didn't even have a chance to sample it today. It would have been a waste for me to eat it at lunch because I didn't even *taste* my sandwich, just shoved it down my throat as fast as I could so I could go right back out front again."

"I'm keeping it in there for tomorrow," said Mona placidly. "It reheats really well. Just don't even pack a lunch tomorrow: there's plenty of casserole. Or bring a little bowl of fruit or something light to go along with it if you want."

I ruefully remembered that I still didn't have a wide selection of food at my house. At the grocery store, I'd been more focused on getting dinner than replenishing the stock in my kitchen. But I wasn't working late tomorrow, so I could run by the store on my way home if I came up with a grocery list now.

After Mona and Luna left, the library became even quieter. Usually Linus was still there, reading up on something interesting in the nonfiction stacks, but he'd apparently gone home to play with Ivy. There were also usually a few patrons who liked to come to the library after work and answer emails and read magazines, but they weren't there, either.

I'd asked the staff to name some of their favorite books of all-time for the Fitz's Picks picture and so I spent about fifteen minutes pulling those off the shelves and arranging them on a table. Then I went looking for Fitz, who was proving surprisingly elusive.

I finally found him in the children's section with the same little boy I'd seen him with previously. This time I was determined not to startle him away. "Hi there," I said with what I hoped was a warm smile. "I'm Ann. Looks like you and Fitz are really hitting it off."

The boy nodded shyly and kept his eyes focused on the cat, who was all curled up on his lap and purring contentedly. "We're friends."

"That's great. He's my friend, too," I said. I glanced around to see if the boy's mom or dad were anywhere around, but they were nowhere in sight.

The boy must have noticed I was looking around because he quickly said, "My grandmother is reading magazines in the grown-up section."

"That's good. I've seen you here before, haven't I? What's your name?"

He quietly said, "Tom. It's really Thomas, but everybody calls me Tom." He looked at me curiously. "Does Fitz stay here at the library all night? Even when everybody goes home?"

I shook my head. "He did for a little while, but then I thought it would be better for him to come home with me at night." I was going to say that Fitz was lonely at the library by himself, but I chose the more-truthful answer. "I live alone and Fitz helps keep me company at night."

Tom nodded solemnly. "That's good. It's not good to be alone."

Since I didn't know Tom, I asked, "I don't think I've seen you at the library except for that one time. Are you new here in town?"

He nodded again. "I moved here to live with my grandmother." He paused. "It's just that I don't know anybody in Whitby at all."

"It can be hard to meet people, can't it? Do you like it here at the library?"

"It's pretty cool," he said diffidently. "I really like Fitz."

I said, "Do you remember the lady who works here? She left just a little while ago."

He tilted his head to one side. "The one with the purple and green hair?"

"The very one. She has a whole bunch of programs for kids here at the library. Maybe I can give you and your grandma some information about them and you can choose one to try out. It could be a good way for you to make some friends. And lots of kids come to the programs because Luna makes them fun."

His large eyes lit up. "Lots of kids come?"

"That's right. And she does a lot of different things. One time she had the science museum from another town come by and they brought different kinds of snakes and insects for everybody to see."

Tom said slowly, "That would be good. At my school, everybody already has friends."

I felt a little twinge of hurt for him, remembering my own days of trying to make friends in a new school in a new town when I'd moved here to live with my great aunt. "Maybe you'll see some of them here and have the chance to learn more about them. I bet a lot of those kids would like to have *more* friends. It's not like there's a limit to the number a person can have."

An older lady with a walker and a sweet smile came up to us and I introduced myself. "I mentioned to Tom that I could give you both a calendar with some of the upcoming programs for kids. Luna is our children's librarian and she puts together some fantastic events."

Tom's grandmother was interested and we chatted more for a few minutes before she and Tom left. Tom turned around and gave Fitz and me a wave before he left, which made me smile.

I headed to the circulation desk and helped a few patrons with their books. Then my cell phone rang and I saw it was Burton. I glanced around to make sure no one was around and then answered it.

"Hey," he said briskly, "I did find some old records on that day. Good thing the chief at the time made sure his files were organized. From what I was able to learn, it looks like they were very suspicious about the drowning. The kid wasn't too far from shore and it seemed like somebody should have at least had wet clothes in the group from trying to help out. But they couldn't get any information from anybody there, so they had to let it go."

"Did they have a particular suspect in mind? Out of the group, I mean? Luna made it sound like some of the kids weren't even in the area when it happened."

"Whatever Luna knows must have been hearsay because the cops weren't able to get *anything* out of those kids. Yeah, there were paddleboats and things on the scene like some of them may have been out of earshot. But they were all very tight-lipped about whatever happened so the case had to be dropped after a while."

"Okay, thanks for checking into that. I know that probably didn't have a lot to do with your investigation."

"Not a problem. Like I said, you never know when there might be a connection."

He hung up and I stuck my phone on the shelf behind the circulation desk and headed off to finally take the Fitz's Picks photos.

Fitz was, as usual, very cooperative as a cat model when I set him up with the books. I did get one of his cat toys out of the closet at one point, though, when he started looking drowsy. Although reading sometimes makes me sleepy too, I was trying to promote these books as exciting, not soporific. Soon his eyes were huge and his tail was twitching and he was thoroughly engaged with the toy. The trick was to wiggle the cat toy, keep the toy out of view of the camera, and take a picture all at the same time.

By the time I'd finished, I glanced up at the clock. Then I narrowed my eyes and looked again. Was it really past nine?

I took a quick stroll around the library to make sure there were no patrons who'd *also* lost track of time. I grabbed the cat carrier from the breakroom and walked toward the front desk. I realized I hadn't had my phone on me for the last hour or more, so connected with the device again, retrieving it from behind the circulation desk and checking for messages.

Luna had left one and I frowned as I read it. In typical Luna style, it was something of a stream of consciousness. There were some random comments about Wilson's and Mona's interactions at the library today and then she stated: *by the way, I asked my mom and I was wrong. It wasn't Felicity and Scott who were close when their friend died. It was Grace and Scott.*

Grace had been near when her friend drowned. But did it really matter, in the case of a tragic accident? It simply meant she'd probably been eager to get away from Whitby and leave all the sadness behind her—and she had. And quickly become involved with what appeared to have been a very wealthy man with perhaps a fairly limited view on ethical investments.

Then I remembered something else. Scott and Grace's conversation on the boat when I'd been waking up from my nap. Scott knew something then—something about Grace. It could have been how Grace's husband made his money. After all, that fact could be really damaging to her locally. But what if it was something different? What if Grace had somehow been culpable in the drowning at the lake when she'd been in high school?

Which was when the library doors opened and Grace rushed in. I tried to maintain a calm, friendly smile when a cold shiver was making its way up my spine. "Hi, Grace."

Chapter Twenty

A car door slammed in the parking lot outside and Grace paled and turned her head. "Can we lock these doors?" she hissed at me. "He followed me here."

I didn't know why Grace was scared and why she wanted to be locked in with me. But after seeing the look on her face, I hastily moved toward the door, whether to lock it or to run out, I wasn't sure. But before I could get there, the doors opened and Kyle bolted through them.

Grace looked frozen and I'm sure I did, too. Because Kyle was carrying a gun.

"Now you've endangered Ann," snarled Kyle to Grace. "All you ever think about is yourself."

Grace gave me an apologetic wince. "Sorry. I saw you were still here and Kyle was following me."

My mind was whirling.

"How did you know?" she asked Kyle, her voice flat.

"I didn't. Not for a while." He gave a short laugh. "Scott even *told* me and I didn't believe him."

I wasn't sure how to get out of this, but I felt if I could buy myself some time, I might have a better shot at it. I worked hard to steady my voice and said, "You're talking about your girlfriend's death."

Kyle looked at me. "You know about it too?"

I shook my head. "Not really. Just the basics." But I was starting to get a much clearer picture suddenly.

I cleared my throat. "Grace was present when your girlfriend died."

"Amber," said Kyle in a flat voice.

I tried to keep my voice even. "When Amber drowned. You and the others were somewhere out on the lake, but Scott and Grace stayed behind with your girlfriend. Everyone thought it was an accident."

"The police called it an accident," said Grace in a husky, frightened voice.

"It wasn't. It wasn't her time to go. You could have saved her." Kyle's face was blotchy with anger.

A mulish expression crossed Grace's features. "No. No, I couldn't have."

"Scott said you could have," said Kyle.

Grace gave a scoffing laugh. "You mean right before you killed him? I guess he would have said anything."

While they were focused on each other, I stepped just slightly back away from them.

Kyle said, "That's what I thought at the time. Then I discovered something that made me realize he was telling the truth all along."

Grace stared wordlessly at him.

Kyle continued, "When I was helping Scott's family clear out his things, they told me they'd found out some things about him. They weren't sure how to process it." He stared coldly at Grace. "If you couldn't have helped Amber, why were you paying him money every month?"

Grace looked confused, but I could tell she knew exactly what Kyle was talking about. "I don't know what you mean."

"You were *paying him* money to stay quiet about letting Amber drown."

Grace said quickly, "I was paying him money to help him with his finances. He was having money troubles."

Kyle shook his head, stony-faced.

Grace took a deep breath. "You're right, Kyle. Scott was blackmailing me. But only in the last year, when he went broke. And that's the same kind of arrangement we can have, you and I. I understand you need money, too. And I have it to give."

The red splotches on Kyle's face grew even more pronounced and again I slipped backwards a bit.

He seethed, "You think that's what I care about? Money? I care about justice. I care about what happened to Amber."

Grace lifted a shaky hand. "And I totally get that, Kyle. Look, you and I have known each other for years. Even though I know you cared about Amber, money doesn't hurt." She gave a hoarse chuckle. "Believe me, I found that out. It may not bring happiness, but it sure can make life easier."

Kyle was looking uncertain now and Grace went on, "Killing me isn't going to bring Amber back. And turning down money won't, either."

Kyle shook his head angrily and a look of impatience flashed across Grace's face. "Don't act as though you're too ethical to take money. You killed Scott. And he was your best friend."

"Until he stopped acting like one."

There was a long pause and I tried to keep the conversation going. I cleared my throat. "The final straw must have been Felicity."

"There were lots of final straws." Lines of exhaustion were etched into Kyle's face.

Grace made a restless movement and Kyle quickly trained the gun on her until she stilled again.

"How did you find out what happened to Amber?" Grace's expression was somber.

"Scott told me." Kyle saw Grace's look of surprise and shrugged. "He was totally wasted by then and running his mouth. I complained about him chasing Felicity. He said in this really cocky voice that maybe *she* was chasing *him*." He noted our disbelieving looks and said bitterly, "Yeah, that's what I said, too. Felicity didn't want anything to do with Scott and I told him that. But then he said my high school girlfriend had been chasing him."

I could just imagine Kyle's fury at that.

"What's more," added Kyle coolly, "Scott claimed that's why you let Amber drown, Grace."

Grace stared at him.

"That's right—because of petty jealousy. Amber was flirting with Scott while I was out on the lake with everyone else. And when she went swimming and started struggling, you just watched her drown." Kyle's eyes blazed.

Grace kept her voice carefully even. "Kyle, let's talk about this. You can name a price. I know your mother could probably use a hand financially, too. We can make this work out."

Kyle gestured at me. "But Ann knows about it. Which is all your fault. And I liked her—you've made things even worse by deciding to come here when you saw I was following you. You should have just gone home, Grace."

I felt a chill go up my spine at hearing myself referred to in the past tense.

"She already knew before I came here," protested Grace. They both turned to me. "Didn't you? I had a phone call a little while ago from someone on the library board." She gave me a tight smile.

I shifted on my feet. "Oh?"

"I have a couple of friends who serve on the board. Apparently this one received a phone call from your director here that the board needed to meet to discuss my gift to the library. That you had some information that the board needed to hear." The tight smile was totally gone now.

That was Wilson for you. Sounds like he'd thrown me under the bus in the process.

Grace continued, "My friend said that Wilson made it sound as if he didn't entirely know what the issue might be, but that you were to explain it to the board when they met."

A point he hadn't shared with me.

I said carefully, "Wilson didn't tell me that was the case. I did raise some concerns with Wilson and he felt it would be best under the circumstances if the board were convened to discuss your donation. "I just know Wilson and he likes to steer clear of controversy at all costs. Especially when it involves the reputation of the library. Once I realized the source of your husband's income, I knew I needed to let Wilson know, in case that made him think differently about the donation."

"What was there to discuss? I gave money to the library. Wilson gave every indication of being totally delighted with it. In fact, he was falling all over himself to not only accept the gift, but to have you and Luna go out to lunch with me at every opportunity, probably hoping you could procure even more."

"And that was your concern. The source of the income." Grace's voice was flat.

"That was it."

"Right." Grace looked at Kyle. "She's not telling the truth . . . I know it was more than just my husband's income." She turned back to me. "I had the feeling you weren't asleep on the boat. Scott was stupid to say anything with other people around. Or reckless. Or maybe he just didn't care, I don't know. But the first rule of blackmailing is to keep the secret, right? I mean, unless the victim doesn't pay up." Her eyes were hard as she turned to Kyle. "Like I said, just get rid of her and then you and I can come up with an arrangement."

Kyle hesitated and then found some resolve and lifted his gun, pointing it at me.

Grace lunged for the cat carrier and swung it at Kyle hard. The gun flew out of his hand and he went down and Grace turned to reach for the gun.

Which was when a voice that was usually very soft said harshly, "Stop!" This command was accompanied by frantic barks.

Grace whirled to see who it was and to also see what was causing the chorus of deep-throated barking. I didn't care *who* or what my savior was, instead taking the opportunity to grab a nearby library cart full of books to be shelved. I rammed it at Grace as hard as I could. Then I picked up Kyle's gun, and with my other hand dialed Burton's number.

Then I looked up to see who'd gotten me out of my jam. Although by now, I'd already figured it out.

Sure enough, there were Linus and Ivy, standing threateningly over Grace. Well, Linus was looking as threatening as it was possible for mild-mannered Linus to look, and Ivy, who'd picked up on the fact her new owner was quite upset, was *definitely* looking threatening.

Chapter Twenty-One

I breathlessly gave Burton the low-down and hung up. After a moment's hesitation, I called Wilson, too. He listened intently and curtly said, "On my way," before I'd even had the chance to finish what I was saying.

I grinned shakily at Linus and said, "I'm so grateful that you're here that I won't even ask what you're doing here."

Linus, looking a little shaky himself, gave me a small smile. "I thought I'd just walk by with Ivy while I was taking her on her last walk of the day. I knew no one would be here, but the library is my favorite place. I saw lights and could see you inside. And there were cars out in the parking lot that I didn't recognize. I thought maybe you were having trouble with one or more of the patrons."

We looked at Grace and Kyle, who were both still fuming silently on the floor.

"In a manner of speaking," I said.

Burton jogged into the library, looking at Ivy with surprise and then looking at Grace and Kyle and shaking his head.

"I want a lawyer," said Grace immediately.

"And you shall have one," said Burton, his voice dripping with courtesy. "I would say that's an excellent idea, considering the sort of trouble you're currently facing. I'm going to read you both your rights and put some cuffs on you. Considering the fact you've both apparently been unpredictable tonight." Burton glanced over at the cat carrier and at the books scattered from the shelving cart. He carefully read Grace and Kyle their Miranda warnings and handcuffed them as Ivy the dog watched with great interest.

Wilson burst in and I blinked, having never seen him without his omnipresent coat and tie. He instead wore what was apparently his version of casual wear: old, baggy khaki pants and an untucked button-down shirt.

He stared at the scene in front of him, which must have resembled something out of his worst nightmare. There was a large dog in his library. There was a library donor in handcuffs. A frequent patron of the library was slumped on the floor. And his research librarian appeared to have narrowly escaped some sort of catastrophe involving either a cat carrier or a book cart.

He chose to focus on the donor. Wilson gave her a disapproving and disappointed look. "I hope you know we won't be able to accept your gift to the library. Under the circumstances." He glanced around again at the chaos as if not fully understanding what the said circumstances actually were, but knowing they couldn't be good.

Burton glanced over at me. "Ann, why don't you fill us in a little."

I looked over at Grace. "You were right. When we were on the boat, I *wasn't* asleep. I was awake and heard part of your conversation with Scott."

"That idiot," she muttered.

"I didn't really think anything much about it until today. After all, the conversation could have been about almost anything. Then, today, I wondered if maybe it had to do with the source of your husband's income."

Grace gave a short laugh. "Do you think anybody really cares about that? Money talks."

Wilson's brows knit together. He said irritably, "They *do* care about it."

I continued, "People are sensitive to it. That pharmaceutical company completely misrepresented the abuse potential for the drug and contributed to the epidemic. But you weren't one who cared about that. What you cared about was something that happened long ago . . . and here locally. Something that could really tarnish your image in Whitby and make it impossible for you to be able to stick around."

Linus and Wilson looked very curious. Burton looked as if he had a good idea what it might be about. Grace was practically snarling at me. Ivy was definitely snarling at Grace.

I said for the benefit of Linus and Wilson, "There was a tragedy that happened when Grace and the others from the party were in high school. At least, it was definitely treated by the town as a tragedy. The police department at the time had their own questions, but there was no proof that any member of the group had anything to do with the young girl's drowning. However, Amber was apparently found not far from the lake's shoreline, raising questions about whether someone could have potentially helped rescue her."

"And Grace was responsible for that drowning?" Wilson's face was horrified. I'm sure he was imagining Grace's name on the community room and what a lucky escape he'd had.

"Apparently, she was indirectly responsible," I turned to Grace. "Maybe you could fill us in."

Grace shrugged. Apparently, a desire to defend herself was winning out over her earlier request for a lawyer. "I did *not* go out into the lake and hold Amber under water."

Burton said, "But you didn't help her, either, did you?"

Grace shot him a look. "She might have drowned me out of desperation. People who are drowning do that."

Kyle swore under his breath and his eyes glared daggers at Grace.

"And you didn't get any help," said Burton. "It would have been hard for a single struggling swimmer to pull down two friends."

Grace said, "I was frozen. I couldn't believe what was happening." She glanced over at Kyle, who was still furiously staring at her. "Everyone else was gone, canoeing on the lake. And Scott took off to use the park's restroom, although really he was trying to get away from the yellow jackets that were buzzing around us because of our soft drinks."

Burton said, "You know, the funny thing about this is that the police reports say there was lifesaving equipment there on the shore. It was a public beach on the lake."

Grace raised her eyebrows archly. "Life saving equipment? If you mean those foam noodles or preservers, then yeah. I guess so."

I said, "Apparently, Scott didn't seem to see things the same way you do."

"So here's the thing with Scott," said Grace in a suddenly chatty tone as she leveled her gaze at me. "Once he saw how successful I'd become and once his own fortunes changed, he decided he had a problem with what happened."

"Success by scurrilous means," muttered Wilson gloomily.

Grace ignored him. "He thought I should have done something, but he didn't tell the police or anybody else. I was just as upset as anybody that Amber was dead. She was our friend. It scarred us all, believe me. And he wanted to dredge it all back up again." She gave a dry laugh and Ivy barked at her.

Kyle spat out, "For the record, Scott told me you let Amber drown because she'd been flirting with Scott. He knew you had a crush on him."

Grace looked at him coldly. "You mean Scott told you that before you killed him? It's true. I wasn't the Pretty One in high school. I was the one who just kind of hung around with the cool kids and they probably just tolerated me because I helped them with their homework sometimes or could crack a joke every now and then. But Amber was a flirt. And when Amber went under the first time, I thought she was just goofing around in the water. It wasn't like she was yelling 'help' or anything."

Burton looked grim. "Drownings frequently don't look like people think they should look."

"What about the next time she went under?" I asked.

Wilson rubbed his forehead as if he was developing a massive headache.

"The next time she went under . . . okay, I might have thought it was a good chance to teach her a lesson. To have *her* feel a little scared or unsure for once. I didn't really realize what was going on," said Grace.

Burton asked, "And the next time she went under?"

Grace shrugged. Apparently, Mary hadn't come back up out of the water after she'd gone under that time. Which must have been what Scott witnessed when he was on his way back.

Wilson gave a shudder. I could only imagine his internal dialogue: this person, who'd almost been lauded by the library by naming a room after her, was capable of allowing people to drown in lakes.

Linus stooped down to rub Ivy. I suspected that was to comfort himself more than to comfort the dog. Wilson still hadn't seemed to completely notice the canine in the room, although Fitz certainly had. He lolled on his back and gave Ivy a come-hither look as if he wanted to play with her.

"So you're saying your actions weren't malicious," I said to Grace.

"Of course they weren't. Not that I expect anybody to understand that, which is exactly why I didn't want any of this to come to light."

Burton scratched his head. "I'm on the side of the folks who don't understand. After all, letting somebody go underwater to teach them a lesson sounds like the definition of malicious to me. But let's move on. You decided to have a party and invite him to it." Burton gave her a searching look as if he was really trying to understand the philosophy behind inviting one's blackmailer to a party.

"He'd gotten in touch with me while I was still just visiting down here and overseeing the construction of the house. At that point, I was just making short trips to Whitby and then heading back north. During one of those trips, he asked me to go out for a drink. And I was excited to do that because I hadn't seen him in ages." Grace's voice dripped with bitterness.

"That's when he told you he wanted money to keep quiet," said Burton.

"He did. And I gave him money. And then he wanted more. Plus, he wanted to come to my housewarming party with Kelly, probably just to torment me. In fact, he was the one who insisted I throw one and really make it over-the-top. His demands were never going to stop," said Grace. She glanced over at Kyle. "You actually did me a huge favor. Scott was starting to get really sloppy. He was drinking, his personal life was falling apart. I didn't really feel confident that even if I *was* paying him, that he'd keep quiet."

Kyle just scowled silently back at her.

Grace said, "You know, Kyle, what really gets to me isn't Scott. Like I said, you really helped me out when you killed him. What gets to me is that you murdered Roz. When we were in school, she was always nice to me, even when others weren't. And I feel partially responsible for what happened to her because I put her in that bedroom. She heard arguing, she looked out of her window, and she obviously saw something."

There was a long pause. Burton asked Kyle, "Did Roz see you hit Scott with the bottle? Or did she just see you arguing?"

Kyle looked tired. "Arguing. But she put it all together. I didn't have a choice. She was going to go to the police."

I asked slowly, "There was one thing I was curious about. Did Scott really break up with Kelly by text message? Or did one of you take his phone and send the message while he was in the pool?"

Grace snorted. "I did it. It was childish and I didn't mean to hurt Kelly by doing it. I was just looking for a way to get back at Scott in just a small way. He would have figured out eventually that somebody grabbed his phone. At the time, he was such a drunken mess by that point that he probably thought he *had* sent the message. I was just so fed up with him at that point that I was looking for anything to make life harder for him. At the time I didn't realize it was going to make her a suspect in a murder investigation."

Burton said to Kyle, "Going back to Roz. How did you know when to show up at her apartment?"

"That was easy. We were all talking about work over dinner and Roz talked about her schedule because it was such a crazy one. Well, crazy for the rest of us, anyway. I think it felt normal to Roz. Anyway, I knew exactly when she left for work so I just waited in the stairwell. Once she came out, it only took a quick shove. I'm sure she never knew what happened." Kyle looked slightly sick, just the same.

Burton said, "And she was dead instantly?"

"I wouldn't have left her to suffer," said Kyle, a faint note of indignity in his voice. "I didn't want to kill her in the first place. But she came to see me and told me she saw or heard something and was going to talk with the police. I tried to tell her she'd just been confused about what she saw but she could see on my face I was lying."

Burton nodded. "And what happened tonight? Why did you show up at the library?"

Grace broke in, "He was after *me*, that's why. Scott, for all his failings in business, apparently did keep good records. Kyle found out I was paying Scott to stay quiet."

Kyle's face grew blotchy again. "Scott didn't have to die. You should have said what happened."

"You're just fooling yourself. That wasn't the whole reason you killed Scott. Face it—you were fed up with him and that was the final straw."

I said, "So once you realized the truth about Grace, you decided she had to go, as well. So you followed her tonight."

Burton said, "And Grace wisely decided to go to a public location instead of home."

"Endangering Ann in the process," said Kyle darkly.

I said, "Grace at least tried to defend me. She hit Kyle with the cat carrier before he could shoot me." At least, I *thought* she'd been defending me. She might have just been using Kyle's distraction to try and get away."

Grace nodded quickly. She was glad to get brownie points however she could, apparently.

Burton asked, "When did you realize you were in danger?"

"When I realized Kyle was following me. He'd been literally waiting in the dark for me to come out of the grocery store. I put two-and-two together then and knew Scott must have told him something before he died or someone else had filled him in." Grace shrugged.

The sound of car doors outside made Burton glance out to see the state police arriving.

Burton said, "And I think that just about wraps everything up for the time being. I'll get you confessions you both can sign at the station. And I'll need to get statements from both Ann and . . .?" He gave Linus a questioning look.

He cleared his throat. "Linus."

"And Linus." He spoke with the state policemen and then led Grace and Kyle from the building to the police cars.

I leaned back against the circulation desk, suddenly feeling exhausted. "Whew," I said softly.

Linus was peering at me with concern in his eyes as he walked up to me. The concern was mirrored by Ivy who licked my pant leg. "Are you all right?"

I was all set to give my automatic 'yes' when I stopped. "You know what? I don't think I am right now." I glanced down at Fitz, who had also come up and rubbed against my leg. "But I think I'll be all right as soon as I curl up with Fitz at home."

"And a good book?" asked Linus.

I gave a short laugh. "I *do* have a good book, but it's probably not the right time to read *And Then There Were None*. Luckily, I have other comfort reads at home. Like anything by Rosamunde Pilcher."

Wilson was starting to look askance at Ivy, a clear sign that he was emerging from his cloud of shock. He cleared his throat. "You won't need to come in tomorrow."

"I'm on the schedule, though."

He shook his head. "Another staff member recently asked me for more hours and I'm sure he'd be happy to come in at the last minute."

Linus said quietly, "If you're all right, Ann, I'll see you tomorrow." He slipped out into the darkness with Ivy, which made Wilson give a sigh of relief.

Wilson looked completely drained. Of course, he already looked very un-Wilson-like since he wasn't wearing his omnipresent suit, but now he appeared exhausted and gray on top of it all. I had the feeling I didn't look so hot, myself.

"I'm sorry for the way everything turned out," I said softly. "I know you were counting on that donation."

"I wasn't so much *counting* on it, as really excited by it," said Wilson in a tired voice. "I was excited by all the possibilities for the library."

I said, "But you made a great point when you said it could represent a starting point for community donations. We've never solicited them before, but we could start. There are a few people here in Whitby who have the ability to donate large amounts but may never have thought about it. And there are others who use the services weekly who might be able to regularly handle small donations. We've just never asked and never made it easy."

Wilson nodded, still looking very gray at the near-miss with library-related scandal, but I could see a spark of interest in his eyes at the idea. I took a deep breath, realizing this meant yet another project for me down the road. "I could put a little footer at the bottom of our newsletter. Something subtle with a link. And we could easily put something small like that as an email signature for official library emails."

Wilson finally joined in, looking more revitalized. "And on our social media?"

"Most definitely." I felt relieved at seeing the old Wilson coming back to life. I added, "Before Grace came in, I took some great pictures of Fitz with his book picks."

Wilson looked even better at this, his eyes getting sharp again. "Perfect. Maybe you could email them to Luna tomorrow and she could post them on social media and make print-outs for around the library."

"Will do," I said.

I stooped down to turn Fitz's abused cat carrier upright and opened its door to coax him in. As usual, he trotted right in, knowing he'd come home with me.

Wilson said in a bemused voice, "Do you think Mona will be coming to the library tomorrow? Luna's mother," he added, in case I didn't know.

"Probably. She usually comes several days a week so she won't be stuck at home by herself." I gave him a curious look and he flushed.

"Don't you think she's spending rather a lot of time here? Would she perhaps be interested in taking breaks from the library and going out for a coffee from time to time?" His voice was stiff and hesitant.

The headline for me is that Wilson was suggesting that *he* might leave the library. Aside from scheduled days off and board meetings, he rarely if ever left the premises. I recovered from the shock at the suggestion that he might and said equally carefully, "I think she'd love that. She seems to be a social person and Luna can't really get away during the day. A change of scenery and a good cup of coffee would really make her day, I bet." Plus time with Wilson.

He nodded, thinking this through. "Maybe I'll ask her tomorrow."

"Great idea." Good thing Luna was a night owl. I could text her and let her know that she needed to bring Mona to the library tomorrow at all costs. And maybe Luna could even give her mom a heads-up that Wilson was mulling coffee over.

As I carried Fitz to my car while Wilson locked up, I realized this meant even Wilson was having more success romantically than I was.

I put Fitz in the car and then hesitated. I pulled out my phone and before I could overthink it, sent a quick text to Grayson.

Having an unexpected day off from the library tomorrow. Want to take that hike?

About the Author:

Elizabeth writes the Southern Quilting mysteries and Memphis Barbeque mysteries for Penguin Random House and the Myrtle Clover series for Midnight Ink and independently. She blogs at ElizabethSpannCraig.com/blog, named by Writer's Digest as one of the 101 Best Websites for Writers. Elizabeth makes her home in Matthews, North Carolina, with her husband. She's the mother of two.

Sign up for Elizabeth's free newsletter to stay updated on releases:

https://elizabethspanncraig.com/newsletter/

This and That

I love hearing from my readers. You can find me on Facebook as Elizabeth Spann Craig Author, on Twitter as elizabethscraig, on my website at elizabethspanncraig.com, and by email at elizabethspanncraig@gmail.com.

Thanks so much for reading my book...I appreciate it. If you enjoyed the story, would you please leave a short review on the site where you purchased it? Just a few words would be great. Not only do I feel encouraged reading them, but they also help other readers discover my books. Thank you!

Did you know my books are available in print and ebook formats? And most of the Myrtle Clover series is available in audio. Find them on Audible or iTunes.

Please follow me on BookBub for book recommendations and release notifications: https://www.bookbub.com/profile/elizabeth-spann-craig .

Interested in having a character named after you? In a preview of my books before they're released? Or even just your name listed in the acknowledgments of a future book? Visit my Patreon page at https://www.patreon.com/elizabethspanncraig .

I have Myrtle Clover tote bags, charms, magnets, and other goodies at my Café Press shop: https://www.cafepress.com/cozymystery

If you'd like an autographed book for yourself or a friend, please visit my Etsy page.

I'd also like to thank some folks who helped me put this book together. Thanks to my cover designer, Karri Klawiter, for her awesome covers. Thanks to my editor, Judy Beatty, for all of her help. Thanks to beta readers Amanda Arrieta and Dan Harris for all of their helpful suggestions and careful reading. Thanks, as always, to my family and readers.

Other Works by the Author:

Myrtle Clover Series in Order (be sure to look for the Myrtle series in audio, ebook, and print):

Pretty is as Pretty Dies
Progressive Dinner Deadly
A Dyeing Shame
A Body in the Backyard
Death at a Drop-In
A Body at Book Club
Death Pays a Visit
A Body at Bunco
Murder on Opening Night
Cruising for Murder
Cooking is Murder
A Body in the Trunk
Cleaning is Murder
Edit to Death
Hushed Up
A Body in the Attic (2020)

Southern Quilting Mysteries in Order:

Quilt or Innocence
Knot What it Seams
Quilt Trip
Shear Trouble
Tying the Knot
Patch of Trouble
Fall to Pieces
Rest in Pieces
On Pins and Needles

Fit to be Tied

Embroidering the Truth (2020)

The Village Library Mysteries in Order:

Checked Out

Overdue

Borrowed Time (2020)

Memphis Barbeque Mysteries in Order (Written as Riley Adams):

Delicious and Suspicious

Finger Lickin' Dead

Hickory Smoked Homicide

Rubbed Out

And a standalone "cozy zombie" novel: Race to Refuge, written as Liz Craig

Manufactured by Amazon.ca
Bolton, ON